TRUTH OR LIE

The Secret Pack Trilogy

Hide or Die
Fight or Fly
Truth or Lie

The Packverse Trilogy

All for Knot: Book One
All for Knot: Book Two
Knot for Sale

The Knot Playing Fair Trilogy

Knot Playing Fair: Book One
Knot Playing Fair: Book Two
Knot Your Victim

TRUTH OR LIE

EMBER BLAZE

Truth or Lie (Secret Pack, #3)

Copyright 2022 by OtherLove Publishing, LLC

ISBN: 978-1-955073-32-5 (paperback)

For information, contact the publisher at
www.otherlovepublishing.com/contact/

First Edition: April 2022

Author's Note

Secret Pack is a human omegaverse trilogy where the main character doesn't have to pick one person in the end. It features protective alphas and the omegas who love them, but no shifters. The series is intended for a mature audience.

Table of Contents

PREFACE

In which the author over-shares:

So… here we are at the end of the series. I struggled badly with this book, a good chunk of which was already written when Russia invaded Ukraine, precipitating a humanitarian and political crisis that grows deeper day by day. I questioned (and still do) whether it was wise to publish a story set partly in Russia and Belarus with Ukrainian side characters—because this is not a deep, well researched dive into Eastern European history. It's a set piece, existing solely because I thought it would be cool to place an omegaverse book in an alt-1980s soviet era setting, and I didn't foresee Eastern Europe becoming a powder keg in 2022.

If I were a Ukrainian (or an informed Russian) and I read this book, I'd be offended as hell that some ill-informed American idiot decided to set a story about social justice and polyamorous group sex in this part of the world, while my countrymen were dying by the thousands.

However, if I were a reader who'd read and enjoyed the first two books, I'd also be pissed beyond belief if the author threw up her hands and said, "Sorry, writing this book feels insensitive, so you'll just have to live with the series being abandoned on a massive cliffhanger. Oops."

The only thing I could think of was to publish it anyway, but try and use it to make a positive difference in the world. To that end, for the first 90 days of publication (April 1st through June 30th, 2022), I will donate 50% of gross royalties on this book to the Ukrainian Red Cross.

That doesn't sound like much, and it's not. This isn't a series that's been popular or made money—it's deeply in the red as of this writing. But it will probably result in a few hundred dollars sent toward helping people who are in desperate need of help. And frankly, that's the best option I could come up with.

To the readers who've purchased or borrowed the first two books in this series—thank you.

To anyone whom I've inadvertently harmed by writing this story the way I did—I'm so terribly, terribly sorry. I can't imagine what you're going through in this horrific situation. I only hope that my small gesture of goodwill goes some way toward mitigating any harm I've caused.

ONE

Leona

THE RED LIGHT on the video camera stared at me, unblinking. I stared back, keeping my voice strong and clear as I delivered the carefully scripted speech. My hair and makeup were perfect. My message was vital and just.

"In conclusion, I ask every single one of you who are watching this message to look inside your hearts," I said. "Ask yourself whether allowing alphas and omegas the same basic human rights as betas in any way diminishes your own rights and freedoms. You may find that the opposite is true—that you are not truly free until all human beings are free."

Lifting my chin, I willed the unseen millions of future viewers to think seriously about my words… challenging them to look into my eyes and believe I, as an unregistered omega, wasn't as human as they were.

"That's a wrap," said the cameraman, in his heavy Russian accent.

The red light next to the lens flipped off, and my shoulders slumped from the straight, commanding posture I'd adopted during filming.

"You don't want to do another take?" I asked, already second-guessing some of my choices in delivery and cadence.

A broad-shouldered figure stepped from the shadows, his gray eyes intent. "No, that will suffice. Thank you."

If anyone had tried to tell me six months ago that I'd be looking for approval from Kostya Nikolayev, the Euro-Soviet chairman of the Committee on Alphomic Suppression, I'd have assumed they were off their meds. Of course, if you'd asked me about a lot of things six months ago, I would have given you answers considerably different from the answers I'd give today.

After a lifetime spent concealing my unregistered omega status and working my way up the ranks of the Foreign Service, I was no longer Ambassador Leona McCready of the UFNA. As far as the United Federation of North America was concerned, I was a fugitive. Somehow, I had also become the public face of the Alphomic resistance. It was a position that would ultimately be no less dangerous than hiding in plain sight as an ambassador had been, but it held more of a chance at making a real difference in the world during my lifetime.

I was hiding away with Kameron Patel, my omega packmate, and our three alphas—Flynn, Alex, and Jax. We were staying as guests at Nikolayev's family estate, located southwest of St. Petersburg. Our host, a man I once would have counted as my people's greatest enemy, had turned out to be our most valuable ally. Kostya Nikolayev was an alpha, and yet he'd somehow managed to infiltrate the highest levels of the worldwide beta organization dedicated to crushing our people underfoot.

His family, dedicated to the fight for freedom for generations, had spread its tendrils through the power structure of Russia and Eastern Europe via political maneuvering and strategic marriages within the great families. As an alpha in a public position, Nikolayev's life would have been much simpler if he'd stayed unattached, or perhaps entered into a marriage with a prominent and trustworthy beta woman. Instead, he'd somehow ended up mated to Rhys Beckett, an omega prominent in the UFNA branch of the alphomic underground.

I'd sworn to myself that I'd get that story out of Beckett at some point. But, however it had originally come about, if it weren't for that unlikely mating I'd be dead three times over. Nikolayev had provided intel and logistical support that had saved me on multiple occasions, all of it done from behind the scenes and presumably at great risk to himself.

Most recently, he'd provided soldiers and helicopters to execute a daring rescue of his mate and two of my alphas after Enoch Sloane, the head of the UFNA branch of the Committee, captured them for torture and interrogation. Sloane knew Nikolayev was hiding something, and he'd long held hopes of exposing his rival as an alpha. The Russian's desperate rescue mission to retrieve Beckett, Flynn, and Alex ended up catapulting the hidden conflict between the Committee and the Alphomic underground resistance into the open—ultimately exposing the extent of the underground's infiltration into worldwide beta institutions.

We weren't ready for open warfare with the Committee—but that wouldn't stop the war from coming if Sloane got his way. For now, our best chance was to turn it into a battle of public opinion, preferably before Sloane and his terrorist allies could turn it into a battle of bullets and experimental, alphomic-targeted chemical weapons.

That was where Kam and I came in. Before I was exposed as an unregistered omega, I'd been a high-ranking diplomat, and Kam had been my attaché. We had established connections in international circles. Not only that, but bringing people around to my side of an argument had once been in my *actual job description*. Beckett and Nikolayev had drafted us into their cause in hopes that we could bring those skills and connections to bear on the underground's behalf.

So far, that meant recording videotaped speeches for release to news organizations worldwide while hiding away in Nikolayev's heavily guarded family estate. In many ways,

Kam and I were currently safer than we'd ever been in our lives. The answer to the question 'How rich and powerful is the Nikolayev family?' appeared to be 'They own half of the property between St. Petersburg and the Estonian border, and can afford their own private militia.'

This dreamlike time-out-of-time wouldn't last forever. Eventually, I would have to venture out from behind the protective walls and security patrols of Nikolayev's estate, so I could meet with leaders on the world stage in person. After months of laying the groundwork, that time was fast approaching—but first, I would have to deal with something else that was approaching even faster.

My heat cycle.

Twice now, I had entered into a no-strings heat contract with my trio of alpha protectors. At this point, 'no-strings' was basically a joke, and we all knew it. Our relationship had more strings than an entire army of marionettes. I had high hopes that this would be the time when we all stopped pretending that we weren't going to end up mated. As it happened, Kam and I had a meeting planned today to discuss exactly that subject.

For now, though, Nikolayev expected my mind to stay on the job... and that was fair enough.

Kam approached and handed me a glass of water. He eyed the Russian warily, a gazelle assessing a lion. "Has there been any further communication from Secretary Fouchet in Luxembourg?" he asked.

"Not directly," Nikolayev said. "I have, however, received a letter from one of his underlings, requesting clarification of Ms. McCready's status and my own position in the Committee."

"To which you replied...?" I prompted, curious how he was spinning his ongoing brutal vivisection of the Euro-Soviet branch. Across the Atlantic, Enoch Sloane's part of the organization was as rabidly bloodthirsty as ever. However, Nikolayev had managed to plant enough moles inside this branch to effectively neuter it with ousters and political infighting, once the shit hit the fan.

"I replied that the Committee is reassessing its objectives, and you are acting as a liaison to discuss alphomic interests with an eye toward normalizing relations with the beta power structure."

That was as nice a way of saying 'the lunatics are running the asylum' as I was likely to hear. The reality was that we were all running around like headless chickens while we tried to stave off a catastrophic worldwide conflict.

"Fouchet's halfway in love with you, Leo," Kam said. "He'll come through in the end."

I raised an eyebrow. "Maybe we should start contacting all the attachés and assistants you've blatantly flirted with over the years," I told him.

"Oh, *please*. I don't flirt," Kam replied. "I'm the picture of professionalism and decorum, and I always have been."

"Maybe we should start contacting all the attachés and assistants whose blatant flirting you've failed to respond to, in that case." I returned my gaze to Nikolayev's steel-gray eyes. "What about Prime Minister Fairbanks' administration? Any movement there?"

"Not yet." The Russian's expression remained impassive, revealing nothing. "They are in a somewhat difficult position after failing to uncover your unregistered status for so many years, while you were in a high-ranking position within the Foreign Office."

"That's true," I agreed. "I suppose I should be pleased that I didn't end up bringing down the entire coalition government when things went bad. Still, Fairbanks has always been a bit of a sympathizer, at least in subtle ways. I can't help thinking he could be the key. If we could somehow pry him loose, he might bring a lot of other leaders along with him."

Levi Fairbanks, the head of the UFNA government, had risen to power on the back of good looks, charisma, and moderate policies. He'd never risked voter backlash by doing or saying anything overt, but he'd remained a quiet bulwark against some of the more extreme anti-alphomic policies that had taken root elsewhere in the world.

"Perhaps so," was all Nikolayev said.

"How's Beckett doing today?" Kam asked, changing the subject.

"He is currently on bed rest, following the advice of my private physician." Nikolayev's tone didn't invite further inquiry.

During his capture by Enoch Sloane, Rhys Beckett had been drugged in a bid to loosen his tongue during interrogation. He'd reacted badly to the injections and gone into an off-cycle heat. Nikolayev's forces had managed to rescue him before the worst happened, but emotions had been running high in the aftermath of the retrieval mission. Maybe Nikolayev had been too addled by heat pheromones to think about the need for contraception, or maybe he'd simply assumed his mate was already too old to conceive. They were both middle-aged, and Beckett was approaching estropause.

However, 'approaching estropause' wasn't the same thing as 'past estropause.' Now, the Nikolayev family was a couple of months away from welcoming its newest member into the world... assuming Beckett's pregnancy went to term. Unfortunately, that wasn't a foregone conclusion by any means. The fact that he was only pregnant with one pup and not a litter was in his favor, as was the fact that the Nikolayev family had access to alphomic medical specialists. Meanwhile, Beckett's age—especially given the stressful circumstances surrounding the conception—was very much *not* in his favor.

"Tell him we'll visit later if he's feeling up to it," I said, wondering if the poor man was going insane with boredom yet. Given what I knew of him, he probably was.

"I will pass on the message," Nikolayev said. "Now, though, I must take my leave of you both. I have a phone conference this afternoon with the Committee representatives from Kyiv and Moscow."

I winced, not envying him. "Have fun with that."

The slight twitch of his lips in response had more to do with irritation than any attempt at a smile. "Quite," he said, and left us alone with the camera crew packing up their equipment.

Kam rolled his shoulders, releasing some of his tension. "Maybe someday I'll be able to share a room with that man and not feel like he's two seconds away from pulling a knife on me," he said. "Sadly, today is not that day."

I knew what he meant. There was no doubt in my mind that Nikolayev was on the same side we were. That didn't make him any less of a terrifying bastard to deal with.

"Something to aspire to," I told him wryly. "So, are you ready to beard the cheetah in her den?"

Kam's deep brown eyes lit with purpose. "Yes, I bloody well am. This whole thing is getting ridiculous."

"Hey, now," I said, twining my arm through his and tugging him toward the door.

"Be fair. Alex has a lot to process, and the kind of trauma she experienced doesn't just disappear in a few months."

Kam sighed. "Of course it doesn't. But if you wall it up and ignore it, then it'll *never* get better. Go on—ask me how I know." The last few words were a low mutter.

I squeezed his arm. "We'll find a chink in her armor. I don't intend to go through another heat cycle with things still in limbo."

Arm in arm, we headed toward the front doors of Nikolayev's palatial manor house—silently girding ourselves to discuss mating bonds with a bereaved alpha. Specifically, an alpha who'd made it crystal clear that she never wanted to hear the word '*mate*' again.

TWO

Leona

SPRING IN RUSSIA near the Gulf of Finland was a capricious thing. Frequently gray, sometimes snowy, occasionally rainy when the temperature crept above freezing. There had been snow blanketing the ground constantly since we'd arrived late in the previous autumn. A steady rainfall two days ago had revealed the first patch of bare earth I'd seen in months.

Today, we'd been blessed with a rare day of brilliant sunshine, pushing the mercury up to something approaching pleasant. I was Colorado born and bred. That, along with years of living in Montreal, had cemented my tolerance for chill, even if I didn't actively enjoy it. Kam, who'd been raised in Kolkata, still despised the cold—but he'd kept a lid on his grumbling when Alex suggested we meet on the balcony of the guesthouse where we'd been staying.

The sheer amount of wealth on display in the Nikolayev estate was staggering. The word *guesthouse* brought to mind a cute little cottage tucked away at the back of someone's property. Nikolayev's guesthouse was a three-story architectural wonder of curving walls, arched windows, stained glass, and modern amenities.

Every room featured a fireplace, and the basement had been dedicated to a massive gym, complete with its own spa. There was a hot tub, a sauna, and even a swimming pool large enough to do laps. I'd counted nine bedrooms, not including the two fully furnished omega nests. The decor was lavish, balancing on the knife's edge of gaudiness. I would never in a million years have associated such a house with the dour Committee chairman.

Not that Nikolayev actually lived here, of course. This was the *guesthouse*. The main house was basically a palace.

Kam and I made our way upstairs to the second floor without meeting either Jax or Flynn. They were probably downstairs making use of the gym, trying to work off some of the frustration of inactivity. Depending on how long it took us to slap sense into Alex, maybe we could join them afterward and watch for a bit.

Kam cut me a sidelong glance. "You're thinking about Flynn and Jax sparring shirtless."

I frowned at him. "Okay, that was mildly creepy. How could you possibly know that?"

He tapped the side of his nose. "You're perfuming."

"Good lord," I muttered. "My heat's not even due for a week yet."

"Welcome to the wonderful world of not taking pheromone suppressors," he said. "You never had a chance to practice modulating your scent when you were young. It will come with practice, I expect."

Kam, a purebred, had grown up with that sort of knowledge. I, on the other hand, had been born to beta parents, and had only presented as an omega at the age of fifteen. After that first, disastrous heat, I'd been on pheromone and heat blockers continuously until last year.

"Damn. That could be a real nightmare during negotiations," I said. "At least, it might be if any of the betas can interpret changes in scent. There's nothing like having every dignitary in the room privy to your innermost thoughts about Adonis belts."

"More like having everybody in the room know that you're horny in general," Kam replied wryly. "It's closer to smoke signals than Morse code, odama. At least it will be to anyone who doesn't know you as well as I do."

"*Smoke signals*?" I echoed, darkly amused by the comparison. "I'm not sure if that's better or worse."

After some discussion, Nikolayev and I had agreed that if we were going to be forced into open conflict with the beta social order, we'd approach it while being what we truly were. Not as the carefully sanitized, beta-friendly version of alphas and omegas, injecting ourselves with a cocktail of drugs so we wouldn't perfume or cycle normally — but rather, as people with complicated lives and relationships, and an equally complicated biology.

Anyone who wished to communicate with me next week would be out of luck, whether they were a king, or a president, or someone's low-level messenger. Next week, I'd be in heat, and therefore unavailable — period, end of sentence.

The idea was mildly terrifying, yet also exhilarating. It was only feasible because I was squirreled away in this impenetrable compound, guarded by armed soldiers and high walls. In a less secure place, it would have been like putting up a neon sign saying *HEY LOOK GUYS, I'M IN HEAT AND TOTALLY HELPLESS — COME AND GET ME.*

Yet, if I couldn't have a heat cycle in peace while staying on the Nikolayev estate in the middle of the Russian wilderness, then I'd never have a heat cycle in peace *anywhere*. I might as well take advantage of the opportunity while I had it.

The guesthouse balcony had been constructed on the roof of the multi-vehicle garage on the ground level. Warmth rising from the heated garage had melted the snow on the balcony's fancy brick floor. Nevertheless, it still would have been a chilly place to meet, if not for the roaring flames coming from a large fire pit situated in the center of the open space.

Three chairs had been pulled into a loose semicircle around the merry blaze. Alex sat in the leftmost seat, staring contemplatively into the fire. Even in such informal surroundings, her shoulders were an unbroken line of tension. Her back was to us, but I harbored no illusions—she already knew we were here. Alex was all alpha, and that included heightened senses. She'd probably heard our approach before we even opened the balcony door. Her obvious tension aside, the fact that she would give us her back like this was a huge compliment.

We crossed to the empty chairs. Kam took the center one, and I took the one farthest from her.

"How was the filming?" Alex asked.

"I think it went well," I said, accepting the neutral conversational gambit. "We might have a nibble from an official in Luxembourg soon."

"Have you spoken with Beckett today?" Kam asked. "Nikolayev said the doctor put him on bed rest. He's probably going to go mental within a week."

"Whelping is dangerous for an omega his age," Alex said, in the carefully flat tone that she used to hide her emotions. "Especially one who's never had pups before. To answer your question, no, I haven't seen him today. I'll go check on him when we're done here."

"We can go together," I told her. "Assuming you don't want to run for the hills after this conversation."

She shifted in her seat. "If it's about your heat, there's really nothing more to say. I've told you before—I can't stop Jax and Flynn from mating you, if the four of you are set on it. Hell—Jax and Kam are technically mated already."

"And we've told *you* before—that isn't the point," I said. I had no intention of losing my temper with Alex... though Kam might, if she pushed him too far. That being said, blunt talk often seemed to be the only way to get her to engage beyond shallow deflections.

Her hard green eyes pinned me. "Then what is the point, Leona? You both want something from me that I'm incapable of giving. That part of me was broken a long time ago."

Alex had mated before, and it had ended tragically. Her former mate was still alive at least—though she was sterilized now, with her mating gland cut out by Committee butchers. I understood that Alex wasn't in any hurry to sign up for a potential repeat of that experience—but that wasn't what we were asking of her.

Or rather, it wasn't what *I* was asking of her.

"Yes," Kam said, his voice low and misleadingly mild. "Please—let's talk about being broken when it comes to mating."

I hid a wince and sat back in my chair, ceding the floor to my packmate. I hadn't expected the gloves to come off quite that fast... yet here we were.

"You more than anyone should appreciate the dangers of this," Alex shot back, never one to back down from a fight.

Kam's brown eyes snapped with reflected firelight. "The dangers? Let's see. Some or all of us might die. Some or all of us might be captured. We might be tortured. We might become victims of the Beta Liberation Front's experimental nerve gas. Perish the thought—I mean, whatever would we do if any of those things happened?"

I suppose I could have warned Alex that when Kam's temper finally reached its tipping point, he played dirty. With the exception of death, everything on that list had already happened to us. And frankly, that no one had died so far was a miracle.

But Kam wasn't done. "And *of course* if you aren't mated to us, you'll be completely blasé about the prospect of our suffering. Just like I didn't give a damn about Jax's wellbeing before I had his bite mark on my shoulder, but now I suddenly care what happens to him because we're *technically fucking mated.*"

This was the reason I usually tried to avoid pissing Kam off. I kept my mouth shut and waited for the fireworks to die down.

"A mating implies an additional expectation of care—" Alex began.

"You've already risked your lives!" Kam's normally quiet voice rose to a shout. "You've done it over and over—for us and for each other! There is *literally nothing more you could sacrifice for us*, simply because we were mated!"

"There's the bond!" Alex's voice rose to match his. "*Damn you*—there's the bond. Another part of my soul that could be ripped out by the roots."

My throat tightened in sympathy at the raw pain in her voice.

"Not with me." Kam's voice had gone quiet again, as he delivered the three devastating words.

His mating gland was still there, but it was useless after what had been done to the rest of his reproductive system in the slave pens. Jax had bitten him during a moment of passion, not realizing that Kam was left-glanded instead of right-glanded. Neither of them regretted the slip... but no psychic bond had formed between them. Kam's body was too damaged.

Alex dragged her gaze away. Her complexion was pale as milk, highlighting the dark circles under her eyes from too many lost nights of sleep.

"I would still feel it," she said.

The flat statement was irrational, in the sense that Kam wasn't magically going to form a functioning mate-bond with Alex any more than he had with Jax. Yet it still cut me to the bone with its utter certainty.

I drew breath to wade into the fray.

"I respect that," I told her. "Mating again—or not—is one hundred percent your own decision. What I need to find out is whether there's a way forward for our two packs. You say you can't stop Jax and Flynn from mating us. But you can—because we're not going to mate members of your pack against your wishes, Alex."

Alex was silent, still looking into the flickering flames rather than at either of us.

"I told the others that you have a say in what happens next, and I meant it," I went on, more gently. "That's why you saying 'I can't stop you' isn't going to be enough for us."

Silence settled over the balcony, broken only by the crackle of burning wood.

"Why do you want this?" Alex asked. "Knowing what you know… knowing how badly things could go wrong… why would you sign up for that kind of pain?"

I did her the courtesy of taking a few moments to think about my answer. Eventually, I spoke, feeling out the words as I went.

"When Beckett was a prisoner of Enoch Sloane, being drugged and tortured… he wasn't alone with his tormenters in that cell," I said slowly. "Nikolayev was living every minute of that horror right along with him, lending him strength even as he mounted a rescue operation. You and Flynn had each other after Sloane captured you, but they could have separated you at any time. And neither of you had anyone on the outside to comfort you. There was no one to tell you help was coming and things were going to be okay."

Alex dragged her eyes away from the fire, looking down at her scarred left hand. She flexed her fingers, bending and straightening them—doubtless taking in the stark red lines etched into her skin where the surgeons had implanted rods and pins to stabilize the crushed bones.

I chewed on my lower lip, aware of how selfish this next part was going to sound. "When the Montreal police dragged me out of my bed in the middle of the night and tossed me into a cell to await Committee extradition, I was more alone than I've ever been in my life. I wanted someone to comfort me more than I wanted my next breath of air. When you came, I didn't believe it was real. If we'd been mated, maybe I would have known that it was."

And if the others hadn't been able to get to me, I would have died a horrible death at the Committee's hands, leaving my mates as distraught as Alex had been after she lost her bond with Irina. Yet I still wanted that connection with a desperate longing.

Like I said—*selfish*.

Kam took my hand and squeezed it.

Finally, Alex looked up. "I can't give you that." Her catlike gaze shifted from me to Kam. "Either of you. But I suppose I also can't begrudge the others a taste of that bond. It's... like a drug, in some ways. I can only hope that they—and you—never find out firsthand what the withdrawal is like when it's unexpectedly taken away."

Kam's hand clutched mine convulsively. I tangled our fingers together and held tight, knowing that Alex's decision wasn't fair to him. Whether he was ready to admit it or not, Kam was falling in love with our recalcitrant female alpha. Her rejection of him had cut him to the quick. I wanted to argue more on his behalf—to drive home the point that she couldn't have that kind of psychic bond with him anyway, so there wouldn't be anything to lose.

Maybe, for her, that wasn't the point. *That part of me was broken a long time ago*, she'd said. Who was I to tell her she was wrong about her own psyche? I ached on my odama's behalf, though.

"I understand," I said, even though it was a lie. How could anyone come to know Kam and not fall in love with him?

"You don't," Alex replied, sounding tired. "And I pray you never do. You should go tell the others the news. I'll check on Beckett and give him your regards."

Kam let my hand drop. "You'll still be there for Leona's heat, though? Won't you?"

Alex shook her head. "I was only present to play referee before—to make sure no one stepped out of line in the passion of the moment. You don't need me around if you're already planning to mate them."

I held my breath. Alex had done a *lot* more than play referee during my last two heats.

"What if we *want* you there?" Kam asked, his tone carefully level.

There was a beat of heavy tension.

"I'm sorry." She rose abruptly, the chair legs scraping on brick. "I can't."

And then she was striding across the balcony, disappearing through the door like a shadow.

"Well, *fuck*," I said, with feeling.

THREE

Kameron

I WATCHED ALEX go with a sense of numbness. Next to me, Leo cursed sharply. Maybe I would have done the same, but I couldn't seem to call the right emotion to hand.

Leo rose and stepped behind my chair, wrapping her arms around me and resting her chin on the top of my head. "I'm sorry," she said. "I'm so sorry, odama. Maybe she'll come around when she's had more time to think about things."

Maybe she would. To be honest, I doubted it.

"We should go and tell the others," I managed. "They'll be relieved she's on board with the rest of it, at least."

I couldn't imagine how awkward it would have been if Alex had been dead set against the others mating us. She was their leader, and Leo never would have forgiven herself if the conflict tore their pack apart.

Personally, I was more worried that the mating bond itself would end up tearing them apart. I'd been young when I was taken away from my purebred family, but not *that* young. I was old enough to be aware of alphomic pack dynamics, and I wasn't aware of any matings where one member of a pack cut themselves off from the rest by failing to join in the psychic bond.

Sure, it had probably happened at some point. For all I knew, it wasn't even that unusual—at age twelve, my sample size was hardly a large one. But did those packs survive afterward? That was the question.

Leo brushed her cheek against mine, scent-marking me. Her lips pressed lightly against my temple a moment later. "Yes. All right," she said. "Let's go tell the others. Maybe they'll decide to take another crack at her, too."

I closed my eyes. "I'm not interested in harassing her into mating either of us when she clearly doesn't want to. I just wish…" The sentence trailed away to nothing, a growing lump in my throat choking off the words.

"That she wanted it on her own?" Leo suggested.

That was *exactly* what I wished for—but I shook my head dismissively and pulled away from her, standing up. We'd held Alex in our arms as she wept for her dead pups. I'd forced care on her when she wouldn't treat her own injuries properly. None of those things obligated her to enter into a mate bond with either of us—especially not when she'd been wounded so badly by a broken bond before.

"It's her decision," I said, with more certainty than I felt.

We went inside, where we'd be warm, if nothing else. I could only imagine what it cost to heat this enormous house during a Russian winter... much less the main house. Good thing money didn't appear to be an issue for the Nikolayev family.

As we headed downstairs, I berated myself for failing to appreciate what we had, simply because of what we couldn't have. We had two alphas who adored us. Both of them would step between us and a bullet without a second thought.

The sound of grunts and thuds reached us from the area of the gym set aside for sparring. All three of the alphas had been struggling a bit during the long months without action, hidden away in relative safety and probably feeling a bit surplus to requirements. They'd all been injured to varying degrees. Flynn had fared the best, though 'best' felt a bit facile when it included being beaten to a pulp and undergoing hours of electrical torture.

Alex's broken hand had healed well, considering. She was still undergoing rehabilitation for it, all these months later. I hadn't seen the whip marks on her back recently, so I had no way of knowing how those had healed.

Jax's bullet graze had ended up being far less of a long-term problem than the experimental nerve agent he'd been exposed to during our earlier capture in Romania. But thanks to alpha toughness, he'd finally overcome most of the intermittent muscle weakness on his left side. He still suffered from headaches, and he probably would for the rest of his life. However, over the last couple of months, he'd worked his body ruthlessly in an attempt to get back to full strength, in a way that made my own gym addiction look like a pleasant walk in the park.

The sparring area was bare except for thick mats on the floor. The alphas were, predictably, shirtless. I'd never been quite sure if that was their preferred way to work out, or if they'd adopted it after seeing Leo's pupils dilate the first time she'd walked in on them.

Not that I was complaining about the half-naked alphas, of course. Omegas were hard-wired to respond to alpha strength, alpha muscles, alpha... *alphaness*. And there was plenty of that on display with these two.

Like Alex on the balcony, they would both have been aware of us since the moment we entered the gym, if not before. Even distracted by their sparring session, Leo's scent would be impossible for an alpha to miss—or to ignore. I adored the fact that she was finally off the blockers, maybe for good. And I was sure I wasn't the only one to hold that opinion.

The pair on the mats puffed up, their muscles bulging as they grappled. They were putting on a show for us, and Leo and I were there for it. Bare feet scrabbling for purchase, they shoved at each other like two bulls locking horns.

Flynn had a slight advantage of both height and bulk. His dark skin gleamed beneath the overhead lights, sweat beading on his chest and arms. Jax had the edge when it came to flexibility. His muscle definition was also something to behold. Leo liked to call him her Viking, with his blond hair, blue eyes, and square jaw sharp enough to cut glass.

It was good to see him nearly back to full health.

Flynn readjusted his grip, aiming for better leverage, and Jax took advantage to duck down, lowering his center of gravity and shifting hard to the right. It should have been a perfect takedown move, but Flynn used his heavier weight to roll them, ending up on top. Rather than submit to the pin, Jax twisted his lower body and somehow managed to hook a leg over Flynn's arm. In a flash, he'd grabbed Flynn's wrist and trapped him in a submission hold.

Flynn grunted and tapped out. "Asshole," he grumbled, as Jax rolled to his feet and offered him a hand up.

"Nice moves," Leo said.

Flynn accepted Jax's hand, pulling himself to his feet as well. He stalked Leo with a smile, backing her against the wall by the door and caging her in so he could press his nose to the base of her neck and breathe in deeply. "Is it next week yet? Because I've got some more nice moves I've been dying to show you."

"I can hardly wait," Leo told him, and tilted her face up for a kiss.

Jax grabbed a towel and used it to mop his face as he sauntered over to join me. "What's up, you two? You've got this whole 'good news, bad news' vibe going on."

"It's Alex," I said succinctly, aware that my face probably looked like I'd swallowed a lemon. "Well, also Beckett. But mostly Alex."

He frowned. "Beckett? Did something happen with the pregnancy?"

"The doctor put him on bed rest," Leo said.

Jax relaxed a bit. "Ah. Okay. Next question. What did Alex do?"

"Let me guess," Flynn said. "You tried to pin her down about the mating, and she said she's fine with it as long as she can stay a million miles away from the whole thing."

"Wow, it's like you know her personally or something," Leo said, laying on the irony.

Jax was giving me one of those piercing looks that saw too much. "There's more," he said. "What is it?"

I sighed. "She bailed on Leo's heat. Apparently, if we don't need her to keep either of you from biting us, there's no reason for her to be there—at least, according to her."

Had that come out sounding bitter? Yeah… it probably had.

Blue eyes peered straight through my skull and into my brain, without the need for a psychic mate-bond.

"I will give you a one hundred percent personal guarantee that she didn't stop and think how that would sound before she said it aloud," Jax told me.

"It doesn't matter." I gave myself a mental shake. "Maybe it's for the best if she's not there."

Spoiler alert—it was not, in fact, for the best.

"You want us to gang up on her?" Flynn asked. Leo leaned into him, and he rumbled a purr as his arms came around her, settling her body against his.

"No, please don't," I said. "We said it's her choice, and we meant it."

Jax's blunt fingers touched my jaw, bringing my face up to meet his eyes again. "It's not you. It's not either of you, Kam. You're worthy of love... worthy of being mated and cherished. But we're all broken in different ways. This is just the shape of Alex's jagged edges, and sometimes those jagged edges can be sharp."

"I know. It's fine," I lied.

Now Leo was watching me with a worried gaze as well. *Wonderful.*

"It's fine as long as your pack can take the strain," she clarified. "Alex can run away from us if she wants to. That's her prerogative. But promise us that you won't let her run away from you, too."

Flynn scoffed. "Run away from us? Where would she go?"

"That's what I'm worried about," Leo said.

"It won't come to that," Jax promised, as if he had any way at all of knowing such a thing. "We won't let it."

"Nah," Flynn agreed. "We won't. It'll work out, you'll see."

And oh, how I envied Flynn's simple and straightforward view of the world.

"Of course it will," Jax said. "We've still got a war to win and a world to fix, after all. Alex would never shirk her duties when there's work to do."

"Things will be better when we're not stuck rattling around this place day in and day out," Flynn added. "We're all going a little stir crazy."

"Speak for yourself," Leo said into his chest. "This is the safest I've felt since I was fifteen."

"This is the safest you've *been* since you were fifteen," I pointed out. "So that only makes sense."

"Come on, you two," Flynn said, throwing a possessive arm around me so I was tucked against his left side, and Leo against his right. "Help us get cleaned up so we can all go and bother Beckett for a bit. He must be bored out of his mind, and I need a distraction from thinking about exactly how I'm going to bite both of you."

The little frisson that traveled down my spine was irrational. In the end, it didn't matter whether or not I carried their bite scars over my useless, atrophied mating gland. And yet, that didn't stop me from craving it with single-minded desperation as my packmate's heat approached.

Two mates. It was two more than I ever thought I'd have… and somehow it still wasn't enough.

FOUR

Alex

"GOOD GOD. YOU look like you swallowed a beach ball," I said, pulling up a chair to Beckett's bedside. "Are you sure there's only one pup in there?"

"So the ultrasound technician assures me," Beckett replied with his usual brand of understated, self-deprecating humor. "Though I did have to sign a form stating I'm not allowed to sue him if it turns out I'm carrying sextuplets."

I forced a smile. Being here at all required an act of will, and it took a surprising amount of concentration to shove aside the bone-deep disquiet I felt in response to the proximity of a pregnant omega.

Repressed trauma, a psychiatrist would say, and they'd probably be right about that. But this was Beckett—the man who'd hauled us out of the gutter and given us a life. A *purpose*. I sat down, reflecting that he looked nearly as out of place in this palatial bedroom as I felt. Beckett's left eyebrow climbed—I'd stayed silent too long.

"Something's happened," he said. "Is it anything that will require sedation to keep me in this damned bed once I know about it?"

I shook my head. "Nothing like that. It's a private pack matter."

He settled back, propped against the pile of pillows at the headboard. "Ah. Well, I suppose I can guess what that means. I'd offer to help, but I don't have a leg to stand on when it comes to dangerous and potentially inappropriate mate bonds."

Looking at this fearless omega who'd mated the most powerful kingpin in the alphomic underground, I couldn't disagree.

"Why did you do it, though?" I asked. "You must have had some idea what you'd be getting into? Or was it unplanned?"

A flash of memory assailed me — Irina, begging for my bite as she writhed on my knot... my momentary loss of control in the face of overwhelming instinct and need. Not for the first time, I wondered what was broken inside me that made me lose mastery over myself when other alphas didn't.

"Not precisely unplanned," Beckett replied. "But... ill-advised, maybe." He took a slow breath, as though considering his words. "There's risk inherent in the act of giving yourself freely to another, no matter the circumstances. We all try to delude ourselves that we can somehow control the future by taking certain actions in the present — or by not taking them, as the case may be. But that's just a pretty lie we tell ourselves, mostly to keep from being paralyzed by the fear of what might happen tomorrow, or the next day, or the next."

"By that argument, everyone should do as they please with no thought for the possible consequences," I said, scowling. "Society would crumble."

"Yes, I suppose so," Beckett agreed. "But the fact remains that walling yourself off from the world doesn't magically prevent tragedies from occurring. It merely ensures you'll always be alone."

Somehow, I didn't think that saying *'yes, that's the general idea'* would go over terribly well, so I said nothing.

"Leona's next heat is coming up," Beckett continued, when it became clear I wouldn't be filling the conversational gap. "Are you going to stop the others from mating her and Kameron?"

"I wanted to stop them," I admitted, feeling my lungs constrict. "Why take that kind of risk now, when things are poised to become more dangerous than they've ever been?"

But Beckett only shook his head.

"You're looking at it backwards, Alex. They want to mate now *because* things are about to become even more dangerous," he said simply. "Fear of lost chances is one of the most powerful motivations a human being can experience."

"Is it, though?" I asked.

He gave me a small smile in lieu of an answer, only to wince a moment later, his hand going to the bulge in his abdomen.

I frowned. "Are you all right?"

"Contraction," he said, his expression smoothing out to a blank facade. "Hence the reason for me being stuck in this bed for the next two months. Anyway, my point is this. You already have a pack. You'd die for them. They'd die for you. If that ever happened, heaven forbid, it would rip part of your heart out. As much as you might like to, you don't live in a bubble, Alex."

It was eerily close to the conversation I'd just had with Leona and Kam. I opened my mouth to say something defensive and probably ill-advised, but the sound of the door opening interrupted me.

Nikolayev stalked in, his heavy brows knit together as his piercing gray gaze fell on his pregnant mate. "I felt that. You're in pain. I'll call the doctor back."

Beckett sighed. "Oh my god. *This* is the reason we never lived together, Kostya—not the damned underground. *Just stop.*"

It should have been amusing, watching the head of the Euro-Soviet Committee fussing over an omega who'd doubtless seen far more deadly battles than he ever had. In any other mood, maybe I could have appreciated it.

I rose from my chair. "I'll give you two some privacy."

Nikolayev barely acknowledged me.

Beckett gave me a final, wan smile. "Think about what I said, Alex."

"Sure thing, Boss." The words slid off my tongue as though I actually believed I'd be able to focus on anything else over the coming week until Leona's heat.

Maybe if I asked nicely, Nikolayev could find me a promising suicide mission somewhere, because the idea of being within a hundred miles of Leona and Kam's nest—while knowing that my idiot packmates would have their teeth buried in the pair's flesh—made me feel like I was about to crawl out of my own skin.

Funny how badly I wanted the very thing that would destroy me if I ever let it happen.

FIVE

Leona

SECRETARY FOUCHET finally came through with a proposal for a private meeting with several officials from Luxembourg and Austria. I should have been ecstatic, but I couldn't be bothered to focus on the details because my heat was coming on. In some ways, it was shocking how little I suddenly cared about world events, simply because of a cocktail of hormones rushing through my veins.

The idea that so much of what made me *me* relied on a few milliliters of biologically active chemicals should have been deeply disquieting. Fortunately, I couldn't be bothered to focus on that worry either.

Right now, I was too busy obsessing about the nest. This was the first time I'd ever used the same nest for multiple heats. It should have been instinctually reassuring, but instead, I was hyper-focused on the fact that I didn't know what we were going to do whenever we finally left the haven of Nikolayev's estate.

Kam and I were fugitives. So were the alphas, for that matter. But even if they hadn't already been outed as underground operatives, they had no money to speak of. They'd been subjugated—slaves in all but name. Only the fragile protection of the military alpha program separated them from the thousands upon thousands of victims of the alphomic slave market. Fair payment for their hard and dangerous work wasn't part of that deal. Beckett might have protected them from the more repugnant legal requirements like chemical castration, but I was pretty sure he hadn't been secretly passing them money under the table.

I paced the nest, chewing on a fingernail as I ran through increasingly unlikely scenarios related to where and how we would live, once we were mated and out from under Nikolayev's umbrella of safety and comfort. Would Alex stay with us, wherever we ended up? Or would our mating drive her away from her two packmates?

A hand reached out and snagged my arm as I waded restlessly through the sea of pillows. Kam was seated on the stylish semicircular couch that surrounded half of the sunken nest. He tugged me onto the plush upholstery at his side.

"*Stop*, odama," he said. "Your brain is going to start spewing smoke out your ears like an overheating engine."

I let out a massive sigh. Some of my tension drained out along with the air in my lungs. Curling against Kam's side, I nipped at his neck and tucked my head against the crook of his shoulder. "Sorry."

He stroked my hair back. "Don't be sorry. Just try to focus on the important things, yes? You're going to be mated." He quickly corrected himself when I drew breath to chastise him. "*We're* going to be mated, I mean. Who could have ever foreseen such a thing?"

It was true. I nodded against his neck. "You're right. Good god, Kam—we're going to have a pack. A proper one." I shivered—excitement, nervousness, and anticipation swirling together in my stomach along with the liquid heat of my growing arousal.

"Yes, we are," he agreed. "They'll be here in a few minutes. Want to see if we can shock them?"

The warmth in my belly surged, overtaking my jitters. "You're on." Thinking for a moment, I straightened away from him and tried to put on a commanding expression. "Clothes off. Get naked and kneel on the floor. I want them to find you eating me out when they open the door and walk in."

Kam rose with a dancer's grace and faced me as he started on the buttons of his shirt. "For so many years, I thought I was the depraved one in this relationship, odama."

I smiled, my earlier cares falling away. "If I'd known how things were for you, I would have embraced depravity long ago."

Gooseflesh erupted across my body, and anticipation washed over me as more and more smooth olive skin appeared. Kam was still ethereally beautiful, scars and all. I drank in the sight of him, watching avidly as his trousers and underwear joined the pile of discarded clothing, leaving him bare to my gaze.

He dropped to his knees in front of me, looking up at me through long, dark lashes.

"Hands behind your back," I whispered hoarsely, letting my legs fall open to make space for him. I was wearing nothing but an oversized T-shirt that smelled of alpha sweat, which left me fully exposed to his simmering regard.

Until the alphas, I'd known next to nothing about sex. Or, rather, I'd known nothing about the ways that sex could live inside the mind, rather than in the body. And, in some ways, I'd known nothing about the omega who'd shared my life since we were both wet-behind-the-ears interns at the Foreign Affairs office.

Kameron Patel didn't want to be worshipped. He didn't want to be adored.

No—Kameron Patel wanted to be put on his knees and used over and over until he was a quivering, exhausted wreck. It was the only way he could escape from the awareness of his damaged body and retreat into the place in his mind where he was still whole… still a sexual being.

The first time I'd seen it done to him, I'd been shocked, even though I was trapped beneath the mindless haze of my heat when it happened. Since then, I'd come to understand that if the goal was to give Kam pleasure, I couldn't simply treat him the way I'd want to be treated. I was an omega, but that didn't mean I couldn't help the others use him the way he longed to be used.

With his hands clasped behind him, Kam shuffled forward on his knees until he could kiss his way up my inner thigh. When he got close enough that the pressure of his lips and the rasp of his tongue became a tease rather than a pleasure, I slid my fingers through the thick, dark strands of his hair and fisted it, twisting until I felt him gasp and shudder.

"Get to work, odama," I said, using my grip to move his mouth where I wanted it.

Kam had a talented tongue, and not just in the sense of diplomatic acumen. I moaned approval as he brushed his lips over me, teasing open my folds like someone teasing open a lover's lips in a languid kiss. I was already perfuming in great clouds of honey and orange blossom. Before long, I might be able to catch a hint of Kam's subtle ginger and lemon, as well.

Until then, I relaxed into the nerve-tingling sensation, letting it unknot my muscles even as a new tension grew inside me. My grip on Kam's hair tightened until he whimpered. He redoubled his efforts, lapping up the slick I was churning out and sliding his tongue up to circle my clit. I gave another warning tug, and his lips closed around my sensitive nub, his tongue flicking rapidly. He sucked lightly, and the tightening spring inside me burst free.

I arched and jerked out my first orgasm just as the door to the nest opened, and the scent of two horny alphas wafted in.

"Holy fuck," Flynn said, sounding hoarse.

"I got tired of waiting," I managed, trying for a teasing tone and only managing breathiness.

"If we'd known what we were missing, we'd have been here sooner," Jax said.

Flynn was already stripping. "Jax, get the toys and the lube out for me. Ginger Tea, you are in so much trouble for starting without us. I'm going to make sure you stay filled at both ends until you don't even know which way is up."

Kam made an approving sound against my clit.

Jax set a small case on the table next to the couch and rummaged around in it. "You can keep our cocks warm while we're taking turns with Leona, Kam. But for now, just keep doing what you're doing while this pervert figures out how big of a plug you can take."

"And keep in mind that you'll be taking that asshole's knot before we're done," Flynn added. "So you'll want to be good and loose by then."

Kam made a choked sound as Flynn kicked his knees wider and knelt behind him, lube in hand. But my odama gamely dove into my pussy again, while Jax shed his clothing and peeled me out of my borrowed T-shirt. He sat next to me, his fingers tangling with mine in Kam's hair. I closed my eyes and let my head fall back, baring my throat to the alpha's teasing nips. I could feel Kam's every twitch as Flynn fingered him open with ruthless efficiency, and my pleasure crested again as I fell headlong into the alpha's care.

SIX

Leona

BEING KNOTTED through a heat was, in many ways, indescribable. Even so, Alex's absence from the nest stung like a splinter embedded in flesh—though I suspected that if she'd been here, it would have been miserable for her. Aside from her general angst surrounding our decision to mate, I'd also decreed that a single birth control method—namely, the injection—was plenty, thanks.

Yes, there was a small chance that it would fail, since nothing offered one hundred percent foolproof protection. However, Nikolayev had access to the good stuff when he had a bit of warning to acquire it... and as strange as it felt to contemplate, I was beginning to soften my stance regarding the possibility of pups. It wasn't just me on my own anymore. It wasn't even Kam and me alone against the world, with our tiny, two-person pack.

We were about to mate a pair of trustworthy, responsible alphas, and Kam had always wanted pups desperately. The way I saw it, in the course of the next eight months, we would either have changed the world into something better for alphas and omegas everywhere, or we'd be dead.

It was something of a moot point anyway, since injectable omega birth control was more than ninety-eight percent effective—as long as you didn't end up with counterfeit drugs like Alex and Irina had. There was very little chance of me becoming pregnant during this heat. If I did, we'd deal with it. I might not have been a model carrier-figure, but Kam totally was. I wouldn't be rearing pups alone, if it came to that.

My first peak was already approaching. The warmth of belonging and care swirled together with the heat of my growing lust, everything combining to steal away my higher brain functions. I was safe in my nest, surrounded by people who loved me. The feel of bare flesh against bare flesh, as Flynn slid his massive cock into me in a slow, rolling rhythm, was everything I wanted out of life in this moment.

Well… it was *almost* everything I wanted out of life.

"You gonna beg for my bite when you come, Sweet Thing?" Flynn rumbled.

His big hands framed my hips, controlling my movements as he thrust into me from behind.

"Yes," I said mindlessly, trying to rock back… to speed up his rhythm until we both lost control. "Yes, bite me! Mate me! Flynn, I want your mark on me… oh, god!"

The words tumbled out without anything resembling a brain-to-mouth filter, nearly falling over themselves in my haste to get his teeth on my mating gland. It must have been working, too, because he let out a full-throated growl and knelt up, manhandling me onto his lap with my back to his solid chest. I cried out as his heavy girth shifted inside of me, hitting a place deep inside that made me shudder against him.

Nearby, Jax lifted Kam's head by the hair, pulling Kam's mouth off his dick. "Come here." He lifted Kam onto his lap on the couch. "You'll want to see this."

Kam looked seriously strung out already, his lips wet and swollen as his glassy gaze met mine. A whine escaped his throat as Jax wrapped a large hand over his half-hard omega cock and pressed teeth to the fading bite scar over his mating gland. His eyelids fluttered, his eyes rolling up to show the whites for a moment before he dragged his attention back to me.

My orgasm coiled tight and hot in the cradle of my pelvis. "Bite me... bite me, Flynn—please!" I begged.

"Gonna make you mine, little omega," Flynn said against the nape of my neck. "Make both of you ours, and never, ever give you up."

His tongue rasped over my gland, and I shook apart around him. He groaned, his knot swelling as he spilled inside of me, and in the next instant, teeth clamped down, breaking the skin.

I wailed, the shivery rainbow burst of pain somehow driving my climax even higher. The skin all over my body tightened, flushing hot, then cold, then hot again. My muscles trembled uncontrollably as I writhed, pinned in place between Flynn's teeth and his knot. I could feel his heart pounding against my back like a drum, counterpoint to my own frantic, fluttering pulse.

His lips and tongue covered the bleeding mark, as he swallowed my blood, his saliva entering the wound at the same time. I clenched around his knot, euphoria flooding me even as beads of clammy sweat popped out on my forehead.

Flynn... I could *feel* him. Not just in my body, but in my soul.

His lips pulled away from my abused flesh, and he rested his forehead against my hair. "Oh, my sweet Leona. You're as beautiful on the inside as you are on the outside."

A sob blocked my throat—too much feeling crowded into too small a space. I couldn't speak, so I shoved all my wonder and dawning awareness of him through the nascent bond. His breath puffed out, tickling the nape of my neck.

Flynn was... *wild*. Uncontrolled in some ways, but tightly constrained in others. His mind was in shades of stark black and white, binary and uncompromising.

This is good.
This is bad.
I want this.
I don't want that.

Overlaying all of his other thoughts and feelings was a single, unwavering directive—*protect*. His consciousness formed a reassuringly straightforward presence inside me, but its newness made it overwhelming.

"All right over there, you two?" Jax asked cautiously. He was still supporting Kam, who had emerged from his sex-daze enough to watch us with wide brown eyes.

"He's inside me," I said stupidly, my voice a breathless rasp.

"That he is. Though you should be glad it's me over here watching, and not him," Jax said. "Because that sex joke practically writes itself. Seriously, though—you're both okay?"

"Halfway there, for sure," Flynn said. "It's so good, Jax. *Really* good. Still need to bite someone else today, though."

I could only manage a nod, agreeing with everything he'd said, but completely overcome by what I was feeling.

"Once the bonds settle, you'll be able to learn how to control them better," Kam said. His tone was faintly wistful.

Of course, my purebred odama was the only one here who'd ever been properly educated in such matters. I believed him, though it was hard to picture this runaway sharing of self as ever being *under control*.

But I was still in heat, and mate-bond or no, my body was following a script beyond the scope of willpower. I was sated and knotted, my first peak past.

"Sleepy now," I murmured, letting my head fall back against Flynn's shoulder.

He immediately started purring, his powerful arms encircling me to hold me snug against him. That unassailable sense of protectiveness rose again, settling over me like a blanket.

"Then you should sleep," he said. Alpha strength supported me, barely jostling the place where we were connected as he settled me on my side and spooned me from behind. "I'm not going anywhere. Not ever again."

Kam slid from his place on the couch and crawled through the sea of pillows to reach us. He stretched down, meeting my lips in a chaste kiss. "Congratulations, odama. May your new bond be a light to guide you always."

I stared into his beloved face, feeling Flynn's affection for the omega leaning over me mingling with my own. "Love you," I said, a single tear spilling over to slide down my temple and into my hair. My body throbbed with the pleasure of being filled, and my heart overflowed with the adoration I was giving and receiving in equal measure.

"I love you, too," Kam said, stroking my cheek.

I closed my eyes, allowing exhaustion to overtake me.

<hr>

If I'd thought sex during my heat was intense before, it was positively mind-melting with a fresh mating bond in place. I'd wondered if Flynn might try to monopolize me, given the chance—but I needn't have worried.

He hadn't been kidding about only being halfway done when it came to biting people. I was currently sprawled across the couch, in that lazy, semi-aware state between the crash following one peak and the rise of the next. Jax's blond head was buried between my thighs, his tongue transporting me unerringly toward nirvana. My head hung over the edge of the seat so I could watch, upside down, as Flynn reduced Kam to a helpless puddle of need.

"You'll take my cock one of these days, won't you?" Flynn asked, sliding a larger plug into Kam's ass.

"Yes, yes, I'll take it! Please... please... I'll do *anything*..."

Something about the desperate edge to Kam's begging kindled a hot surge of need in my gut—never mind that I'd been begging just as abjectly not so long ago. Jax's tongue dragged along my soaked folds, hitting every-thing *just* right, and I moaned as a powerful release clenched my muscles in fluttering spasms.

Flynn looked up abruptly, his dark eyes catching mine. "Huh. So *that's* what it feels like," he said, before refocusing his attention on Kam. "Nice."

Jax chuckled against my sensitive flesh and repeated the movement, drawing a contented hum from my throat and a rumble of approval from Flynn's.

Meanwhile, Flynn seemed to be intent on talking Kam over the edge with his words alone, taking ruthless advantage of my odama's long-buried thirst for submission and sexual humiliation.

"You know, Ginger Tea," he said, "once we've got you all trained up so you can take an extra-large alpha cock, we might just tie you up in the corner during Leona's heats with your ass on permanent display. Anyone who needed a convenient place to bust a knot could just stick it inside you while they're waiting for the next round. Hell, I could even find Leo a nice strap-on harness with a knotting dildo so she could fuck you, too."

"Oh god," Kam choked.

"Ooh, I want that," I agreed, floating along on the crest of another orgasm. "I'd fuck you so good, Kam."

"We'll definitely have to do that some time," Flynn said with satisfaction. "But right now, I'm going to put my bite mark right over the top of Jax's, and you're going to come so hard for me that you pass out."

Kam made a garbled *nngh* sound as Flynn manhandled him around and dragged his head to one side by the hair, his other hand closing around Kam's dick and jerking him roughly.

"Such a pretty little omega toy." Flynn ran his teeth teasingly over Kam's scar. "Our toy now." He locked eyes with me, then bit down hard.

Kam cried out and arched, writhing and struggling even as clear fluid squirted from his cock. I was close to the edge myself, but too enthralled by what was happening to fully concentrate on my own pleasure. After several seconds of jerking and shuddering, Kam collapsed sobbing in Flynn's grip.

Six months ago, I might have panicked, convinced that something was terribly wrong. But I'd learned more about what made Kam tick since then. I knew how much repressed emotion he'd shoved into the dark, cramped space inside his heart over the decades, and I knew how precious an opportunity it was for him to let some of it escape like this, in safe surroundings and with people he trusted.

Flynn held him close and soothed the livid bite mark with his tongue. Kam grew pliant in his arms by slow degrees, until he was completely limp, not an ounce of tension left anywhere in his body.

"Bet you could take an alpha cock right now without even twitching," Flynn said with clear satisfaction, pressing a final kiss to the mark he'd left. He stilled, a furrow of concentration forming on the dark skin of his forehead as he straightened. "Hang on," he said slowly. "What the hell is that? Leo—do you feel that?"

SEVEN

Kameron

I WAS TOO wrung out to move; too wrung out to think. Yet my omega hindbrain still sat up and took notice when Flynn's spicy scent sharpened. He was saying something... to... someone? But I couldn't make out the words, because there was something wrong inside my head.

Or, maybe wrong wasn't the word?

Someone was whispering in my ear. Possibly two someones? They were so far away, though. It felt like I was standing in a long tunnel, and they were at the far end. My eyes had slipped closed as I tried to focus inward. A slender hand gripped my thigh and I wrenched them open again. Leo's hazel gaze bored into mine.

"Kam?" Her voice trembled on my name.

Jax was standing right behind her. Distantly, I was cognizant of what I must look like, sprawled across Flynn's lap with splatters of fluid drying on my belly and thighs. It didn't matter. Something had just happened, and I couldn't quite trust that I wasn't dreaming.

"That's you, isn't it, Ginger Tea?" Flynn asked, with something like wonder.

"Kam, we can feel you," Leo said.

And… it was *them*. They were the ones standing at the end of the tunnel. My breath stuttered and caught inside my chest. Jax crouched next to us, one hand on Leo's shoulder and one on mine.

"What's happening?" he asked. "You can feel a bond forming?"

"It's faint, but yeah," Flynn said. "You two are already mated. Can't you feel it?"

Jax shook his head. "No, nothing on my end. Kam?"

He expected an answer. I moved my lips a couple of times before words came out. "I don't think so?" My voice sounded strange in my own ears.

Leo's fingers tightened on my leg. Her words were rushed. "Jax. Bite me. Right now."

There was a slight pause, and then Jax said, "You think he's piggybacking off Flynn's mate-bond with you?"

"Maybe," Leo replied, sounding unsure.

"That could make sense," Flynn said. "Just like we think your system uses Leo's heat pheromones to help you perfume, Kam."

Jax leaned in to kiss the top of my head, then the top of Leo's. "A second bite's going to hurt a lot worse than the first, love. I still want you riding a sex-high when it happens, so you don't notice as much, okay?"

Leo rolled her lower lip between her teeth for a long moment before giving a reluctant nod. "Okay."

Behind me, I felt Flynn's chest rise as he breathed in, scenting the air. "It won't be long. You're climbing toward another peak, Sweet Thing."

I breathed in as well, still feeling like something huge and warm was wrapped around my lungs—smothering me, but in a good way. I could track Leo's impatience and Flynn's curiosity as faraway echoes behind my own rampaging emotions. This couldn't really be happening, could it? I was broken—not a proper omega anymore, despite what the others said. I couldn't have a real mate-bond.

Could I?

Leo climbed up to straddle my legs, both of us in a messy tangle on Flynn's lap. Her lips pressed against my forehead, then to each of my eyelids, and finally my lips. This kiss wasn't chaste. It was filthy, and it helped me center myself instead of spiraling out of control.

The others would take care of me, no matter what this impossible thing meant for us in the long term. I was safe. My shoulder throbbed with Flynn's bite, and Leo's throbbed in sympathy through the faraway bond. Flynn's mouth closed over the raw wound again, soothing it with his tongue and sending fresh shivers along my overstretched nerves.

It was okay. We were okay. Maybe this was some kind of post-orgasmic dream and not reality, but at least it was a good dream? Flynn was a sharp-edged shadow in my mind, his details hard to make out. But even at a distance, Leo shone so very brightly. I managed to get enough muscle control back to wrap my arms around her and hold tight, kissing her back with everything I had.

⎯⎯⎯◆⎯⎯⎯

Flynn had, predictably, been right about Leo's next peak. It was hardly anytime at all before her hormones took control again, rendering her mindless with need. Jax put her on her hands and knees. She arched her back, presenting for him, and I watched from the shelter of Flynn's arms as they coupled, raw and wild and joyful.

Flynn purred behind me, churning out happy, protective pheromones as fast as Leo and Jax churned out lustful ones. It was impossible for me to obsess and overanalyze everything under these conditions—doubly so, since my muscles still felt like rubber after the orgasm Flynn had wrung from me earlier.

I closed my eyes, trying to track what was happening through the fragile bond, rather than by sight. I could feel what Leo was feeling, but it was still muffled, like there was a blanket draped over the connection. And then, Jax bit her.

The jolt of pain and pleasure sparked along the bond with more clarity than anything else had so far, ebbing and cresting in a rhythm with her cries and garbled pleas of *yes, more, don't stop*. Suddenly, Jax was just... *there*... as though he'd always been there inside me—a storm half-seen on the horizon, companion to Leo's sun and Flynn's shadow.

"Holy shit," Flynn said, taken aback. "This is so wild. You getting that, Ginger Tea?"

"A bit," I managed, taking in the fact that Leo and I had a *fucking mated pack* now... even if it was currently one person short.

But I couldn't afford to think about that. Not now, not when—

Jax gave a heartfelt moan that almost sounded like relief. "There you are. Both of you."

"*Both*? And what am I, asshole?" Flynn asked. "Chopped liver?"

"You're a headache, just like always," Jax shot back. "Get over here, you two."

I crawled to them, drawn by the prospect of cuddling, and winced a bit as my body protested. The burn from Flynn's selection of anal plugs—now safely removed to let me rest—would be with me for a while yet. Flynn followed close behind me. We burrowed into place next to the knotted pair. I allowed myself to revel in the others' muted pleasure at the intimate contact, as well as my own. I still wasn't one hundred percent convinced this wasn't all a fever dream, but maybe—just maybe—I could begin to hope.

EIGHT

Leona

FOR THE FIRST time since Romania, I resented the way my heat hormones stole away my rational mind in waves, rising and falling with every peak. I needed to be aware for every single minute of this miraculous new bond with Kam, but biology wouldn't allow it. After I was knotted, I was out like a light for hours, my body enforcing rest so I could recover for the next round.

It helped that Kam was curled in my arms for much of that time, and it helped even more that I could kind of, sort of, feel his presence through the mating bond we now shared. He was *softness* inside my head—fur that begged to be stroked, or a fleecy blanket to snuggle. Yet, compared to the alphas, his presence still felt terribly weak and far away.

Jax tucked my tangled hair behind my ear as I stretched, returning gradually to wakefulness.

"Hello, Beautiful," he said. "I've been thinking—"

"Always dangerous," Flynn muttered.

Jax sighed. "I've been *thinking* that you should bite Kam too, Leo."

"*Me*? But I'm an omega. Is that even a thing?" I asked muzzily.

"Not really," Kam said, in a tone of voice that suggested there had been extensive discussion on the subject while I'd been out cold.

I tried to knock some more brain cells together. "But you think it might help strengthen the bond?"

"The way we see it, there's only one way to find out," Flynn said. "Can't hurt, right?"

I pondered that for a bit. We were all lying together in a naked tangle. Kam was helpfully right next to me, opposite Jax, with Flynn on his far side.

"I want to try," I decided. "Roll over, odama."

"I should make you buy me dinner first," Kam muttered.

"You're holding all our money," I pointed out. "So that's going to be difficult. I could do your laundry for a week, though?"

"Now *that's* romance," Flynn said, and Jax snorted a breath of laughter behind me. Flynn sobered a moment later. "Might be better to wait until we can get him nice and horny again, though. It's going to hurt."

But Kam shook his head. "No. Do it now—I need to know." He huffed and rolled over, presenting his left shoulder with its inflamed mating gland, Flynn's bite mark still livid against the olive-colored skin. "God. This is surreal," he said.

I laid a hand on his shoulder, suddenly unsure. "I just sort of… get my teeth around his shoulder and bite down? That's all?"

"That's all," Jax said. "Blood and saliva carry the genetic match, or so I gather."

"Omega blood and *alpha* saliva," Kam retorted.

I gave him a squeeze. "Careful, now. Anyone would think you didn't want my bite. A girl could get a complex."

His tense shoulders relaxed. "It's not that, beloved." He craned around, meeting my eyes over his shoulder. "I'm just trying not to get my hopes up. You know how I am about things."

I did. So many times in Kam's life, the worst of all possible outcomes had materialized just in time to punch him squarely in the face. He still had a surprising amount of optimism for the rest of the world, but he had trouble when it came to optimism for himself.

"No hopes," I promised. "Only possibilities. I can still feel you. Can you feel me?"

His brown eyes glowed. "I can. You shine like a star."

I smiled, tremulous. "And you draw me like a welcoming haven. Maybe we'll feel even more, after this."

He smiled back, uncertain, and turned away, baring his neck to me. As an omega, the idea of being bitten played into long-buried genetic and sexual instincts. But the idea of biting someone else felt foreign. I'd been raised as a beta, and… well… you didn't just go around *biting* people.

But I'd kissed and teased Kam's mating gland countless times over the years, so I started there. He was extra sensitive to my touch after Flynn's bite—just as he had been after Jax bit him, way back in the holding cell in Cuba. Rather than performing the *wham-bam-thank-you-ma'am* version of omega-on-omega mating bites, I took my time, seeing how strung out I could make Kam with only my lips and tongue playing against the juncture of his neck and shoulder.

The answer? *Very* strung out.

Unfortunately, there was no question of making him come again—not so soon after Flynn had taken him apart earlier. It took Kam a couple of days to recover from that, even in a nest full of heat pheromones. Flynn's bite had already stopped bleeding under the power of his healing alpha saliva. I steeled myself, knowing that if I held back and didn't break his skin on my first attempt, I'd just end up bruising him without accomplishing anything else.

"Sorry," I whispered, before clamping my teeth around the raw flesh and biting down until I tasted fresh blood.

Kam stiffened, a faint, choked noise escaping his control—but he didn't jerk away as I pulled bloodied lips away from the wound and started licking away at him. It felt... *odd*. Not nauseating like I might have expected, but the action didn't really raise any buried instincts inside me, either.

"Oh," Kam breathed, and I realized that the soft, warm presence in my head felt a bit closer now... a bit more immediate.

"*That's* what I'm talking about," Flynn said with satisfaction.

"Too bad no one really does alphomic-based research these days," Jax mused. "This is pretty interesting."

"I'm happy not to be someone's lab experiment," Kam said breathlessly. "Thanks all the same." He paused. "Though... I suppose if it could help other omegas in a similar situation..."

"Maybe there will come a day when that kind of science is common again," Jax said.

"If so, we can always revisit it," I agreed. "But, Kam! We're mated. I can hardly believe it's real."

"Still withholding judgment on that part, actually," Kam murmured.

I leaned around him so I could kiss him, heedless of the blood on my lips. He winced as I accidentally brushed against the wound, and I pulled back immediately.

"We'll have to tell this hypothetical future scientist that omega saliva doesn't do much for closing fresh wounds," he said without rancor.

"I'm on it," Jax replied, and eased me out of the way so he could get his mouth over the seeping injury. I scooted around to a better position and went back to kissing Kam like his life depended on it.

———————◆———————

Omega heat stopped for no one, although the flavor of it was noticeably enhanced with the presence of the bond thrumming between the four of us. Peak followed peak, each one growing in intensity. Jax and Flynn grew less carefully controlled as the days passed—they could feel our responses directly now, and that eliminated much of the need for constant checking in regarding our well-being.

It wasn't quite a full-on alpha rut. They were still rational, beneath all the growling and raw physicality. But it was sure as hell pretty intense. Through the tentative bond we shared, I could channel Kam's utter contentment at being so thoroughly dominated. I began to truly understand his feelings from the inside out, rather than the outside in. And while I'd never really thought I would share those desires for myself, I was starting to see the appeal.

Whereas Kam relished truly fighting back and being overpowered, I was enjoying a certain extra spark of satisfaction in playing the omega brat. It was such a cliché in many ways, but it was undeniably fun winding Flynn up, in particular. For one thing, his 'punishments' never failed to be even more enjoyable than the crime had been.

As my final peak approached, Kam did, in fact, end up taking Jax's knot while I took Flynn's. I was pretty sure the intensity of the four climaxes echoing through the bond nearly simultaneously was enough to knock me down a few dozen IQ points—possibly on a permanent basis.

Worth it, I thought, and promptly passed out.

———◆———

When I regained consciousness, my heat had broken. I'd been cleaned up and wrapped in blankets, with the nest tidied around me. Two other presences hummed at the back of my mind, projecting reassurance, but with an undertone of sadness.

Two presences.

Not three.

I tried to scramble upright, but my muscles were jelly after our four day long sex marathon. A slender hand grasped my arm, steadying me.

"It's all right, odama," Kam said. "I'm here. I'm fine."

Relief that he was physically all right warred with a terrible sinking feeling in my stomach. "What happened?" I rasped.

A strong arm wrapped around my shoulders, and Jax's woodsy scent surrounded me.

"Your heat pheromones faded. We think that's what was boosting the bond," he said.

I could feel Jax's melancholy and disappointment directly. I couldn't feel Kam at all anymore. Not so much as an echo.

Flynn plopped down across from us in the nest. "I bet it comes right back the next time you're in heat. You'll see."

I stared into Kam's face, aware that my eyes were filling with tears.

He cupped my cheeks and brought our foreheads together. "It was always too good to be true, Leo. The last few days have been something I never thought I'd experience in my lifetime. I did, though—and maybe I'll have more of it in the future. Please don't cry for me."

But it was too late. I shook my head helplessly and fell into his arms, clinging tight... weeping the tears that I knew he wouldn't weep for himself.

NINE

Alex

IT HAD BEEN absolutely vital that I get the hell away from the guesthouse during Leona's heat. Fortunately, there were other distractions available—and Nikolayev's main house had something like four dozen bedrooms, so finding an empty one wasn't difficult.

Unfortunately, the most pressing distraction involved an official visit from a Belarusian official and his retinue. This wouldn't have been a problem, in and of itself. We needed potential allies on the world stage. *Desperately.* The problem—if you could call it that—was that this particular Belarusian official happened to be the mate Irina had used to replace me... and she was here, too.

Mate wasn't the right word. They were married, beta-style, and the very idea made my skin crawl. She'd offered herself up as a *fucking bribe*, in order to cement a political alliance. The moment I learned the details, I wanted to kill Dzimitry Polonsky on sight.

He was the People's Commissariat for Social Welfare, a member of the Council of Commissars on the Soviet end of the Euro-

Soviet Confederacy. In other words, he was a big deal in international politics, and he was in a position to help our cause immensely.

Ripping Dzimitry Polonsky's spine out through his ass because he'd laid hands on my former mate would not be a smart move. Beckett would look at me with dire disappointment, and Nikolayev would probably have me hauled in front of a firing squad or something. On the positive side, behaving civilly toward the man was exactly the kind of psychological self-flagellation I currently craved.

I stood against the far wall of the room like the leashed guard dog I was—spine straight, hands clasped behind my back. The fingers of my left hand ached in time with my heartbeat. I must have been clenching the muscles unconsciously—what a shock. Against another wall, Polonsky's two-man security team watched me impassively.

I'd found it interesting that Nikolayev would allow armed security into his private sanctum. I assumed that meant he trusted his Belarusian ally. Or maybe it was meant as a demonstration of power and confidence. If Polonsky turned on his host, the presence of two security grunts wouldn't prevent him from ending up as a blood smear on the wall when Nikolayev's private army stormed in.

Without my permission, my thoughts wandered back to the guesthouse, and what was no doubt taking place inside. I wondered if my idiot alefs were mated yet. With an irritated internal headshake, I yanked my attention back to my surroundings.

"I believe the risk involved with a small gathering of officials in Belarus is outweighed by the potential benefits," Polonsky was saying. "Chancellor Shevchenko will certainly attend, and I suspect he can bring others on board from Poland and Hungary."

Shevchenko was the Ukrainian official that Nikolayev's omega sister had married under a new identity after Nikolayev fake-murdered her when she was a teenager… because apparently selling female omegas into political marriages was a thing this family did with some regularity.

Nikolayev sat back and tapped his fingers thoughtfully against the polished surface of the massive table. "I agree," he said at length. "It is time to bring our shadow alliance into the light, if only to normalize the idea that some countries are open to change."

"To breaking publicly with the Committee, you mean," Polonsky said in a dry tone. "Though what that even means these days is something of an open question, now that you've eviscerated half of it."

Nikolayev didn't react, beyond the flicker of a gray eyebrow. "I'm sure I have no idea what you mean, Commissariat. All organizations evolve. The Euro-Soviet Committee has merely evolved to see the error of its ways."

"Leaving a trail of dead officials and destroyed careers in its wake, yes," Polonsky agreed. Irina, seated across from him, failed to stifle a soft snort. I stared at the back of her head, trying to dissect the omega-shaped hole in my mind. I had the distinct impression that if I were somehow magically given the power to plug my former mate back into that hole, she would no longer fit. The idea was disconcerting.

"Evolution is seldom kind to the unfit," Nikolayev was saying. "Very well. I agree in principle to a regional conference where we will discuss ways to move forward within a new framework of laws and treaties."

Polonsky wove his fingers together, leaning forward on his elbows. "And may we expect the presence of your new spokesperson at this conference? I must say, she's been garnering quite a bit of attention in the worldwide media over the past few months."

I perked up. Bringing Leona and Kameron out of hiding and onto the world stage had always been a part of the plan, but the timetable for doing so hadn't been finalized until now.

"Yes," Nikolayev said. "One can hardly have a meaningful dialogue about the future of alphomic policy without the presence of alphomic individuals." His gray gaze moved to Irina.

"Indeed. What a groundbreaking concept," Polonsky said, with the deadpan air of someone who was in on a private joke.

"What about the security considerations?" Irina asked, all business.

Again, I prodded at the gap inside me where the roots of our bond had been torn out, trying to find the pain. It was there, throbbing in time with the bone-deep scars crisscrossing my left hand—but I no longer had the sense that it could be eased by trying to force things back the way they had been before Irina's arrest. I wasn't entirely certain what that meant.

Nikolayev caught my eye and summoned me to the table with a sharp jerk of his chin. I forced a mask of professionalism into place and joined the discussion of how best to keep anyone from getting killed, filling in for Beckett as best I could until Nikolayev and I could consult him directly, inside his posh bedroom prison.

———◆———

Afterward, Dzimitry Polonsky intercepted me before I could slip away.

"Monsielle Alex, if I might have a word?" he asked in French, using the non-gendered honorific that had once been preferred for addressing unaligned alphas and omegas.

I paused, caught off guard. "Of course, Commissariat Polonsky," I replied in the same language, uncomfortably aware of my earlier gut reaction urging me to wring his beta neck.

Irina watched the exchange intently, but she made no move to join us as Polonsky indicated a door leading to an anteroom off the main conference room. Interestingly, neither did the two security goons—although they were wearing the perfectly blank expressions common to paid guards everywhere who thought their charges were about to do something utterly foolhardy.

Being somewhat familiar with the experience, I could relate.

Nikolayev hadn't missed the exchange either. His expression warned me not to do anything that would endanger the delicate web of diplomacy he'd been weaving. I steeled myself not to react to any potential provocation from Polonsky, desperately hoping this wasn't going to involve some sort of beta breast-beating over the ownership of a woman.

"How can I assist you, Commissariat?" I asked, in a perfectly flat tone, once we were alone.

He waved the words away and gestured me to sit at the small table set in the center of the room. I complied, figuring the symbolic barrier of a piece of furniture separating us could potentially be useful.

"I do not require assistance. Merely a brief conversation," he said, taking the seat across from me. His features weren't classically handsome, though I supposed they were pleasant enough. He had a prominent nose and an aggressive chin beneath sandy hair and light brown eyes. I wondered what Irina saw when she looked at him.

He isn't a constant reminder of a past I would rather forget, she'd told me, the first time we'd spoken after I discovered she was still alive.

"You are Irina's Alex," Polonsky said, wasting no time in going for the jugular.

I pasted on a tight smile in response. It felt like it might split the skin over my cheeks. "Clearly not."

He dipped his head—a gesture of self-effacing acknowledgement. "Forgive me. I know of no good way to say what needs to be said without dredging up old injuries."

"And what is it that you think needs to be said?" I asked, hoping to bring this exchange to a speedy conclusion.

He met my gaze and held it. "I want you to know that I am deeply in love with your former mate. I'm certain I don't need to enumerate all the reasons why. I would like to think she loves me as well—although the rationale on her end is considerably more opaque."

I'm with someone, she'd told me. *I'm in a relationship that makes me happy. He doesn't make me feel as though my lack of a mating gland or a womb makes me somehow incomplete as a person.*

At the time, I hadn't been ready to hear what she was telling me. I still wasn't, but I suddenly seemed to have less choice in the matter.

"She isn't a beta woman, someone to marry in a church and hang off your arm like a trophy," I said sharply, and probably unfairly.

His brows drew together, sadness visible behind his pale brown eyes. "No. Definitely not. She is a proud omega. One who was treated with utter barbarism by monsters in the guise of men. And since then, she has fought every single day to ensure that at some future date, there will be no more damaged omegas like her. She fights with words and with weapons, with her entire heart and soul. It amazes me daily that she still has room in that boundless heart and soul for me."

I could barely breathe.

Betas lied. They lied all the time—politicians even more fluently than most. But deep in my heart, I didn't think Dzimitry Polonsky was lying.

"As long as she's with you of her own free will, then it's no business of mine," I managed, after too long of a pause.

He smiled—a bit tentative... a bit rueful. "Even if she weren't, she wouldn't need you to snap my neck for me. She already would have done it herself."

And I would *not* find this Euro-Soviet beta politician charming, goddamn it. I *certainly* wouldn't find him likable.

"Then, as I say, it's nothing to do with me," I told him. "I'd tell you to keep her safe, but we both know what a sad joke that would be."

He nodded once, allowing me my fictions. "Sadly, that is true. With great risk comes the potential for great reward, but none of us were ready to have our hands forced so soon. We all do the best we can for those we care about, and fate will take care of the rest." He rose, reaching his right hand out to me. "I won't keep you from your duties any longer. Thank you for agreeing to speak with me."

I shook it—a dry, warm grip—and tried not to wonder who I would be if I didn't have to carry around my guilt over a lost omega and a ruined life.

TEN

Alex

SIX WEEKS LATER we were on Nikolayev's private jet, descending toward a small airport on the outskirts of Minsk. I'd already been proven wrong about one thing. Months ago, when I'd helped Beckett retrieve a broken, red-haired omega from Montreal police custody, I had assumed that Ambassador Leona McCready was gone forever.

While it was true she'd been stripped of her official title the moment she'd been arrested as a fugitive omega, the self-assured, put-together diplomat was back with a vengeance, with her trusty attaché at her side. And god help me, I could hardly seem to look away.

Nikolayev's bottomless pockets had provided a new wardrobe and personal stylists for the pair. Leona was dressed to kill from the top of her stylish chignon to the razor-sharp points of her four-inch stilettos. Kameron's carefully cultivated anchor-style fringe of beard was shaped and edged with precision. His understated but perfectly tailored suit was chosen to complement Leona's attention-grabbing beauty, but not compete with it. Both of them looked like greyhounds eyeing the mechanical hare at the starting gate, ready to spring.

Even so, their intensity covered a hint of melancholy. I knew why. Jax had ensured I knew about what had happened during their mating. He hadn't delivered the report with the kind of cruelty I probably deserved—instead framing it both as pack business and information relevant to our ongoing security.

Kam had been able to form a bond within the heat nest, only to have it slip away when Leona's pheromone production declined. I hoped with all sincerity the pain of feeling that bond evaporate had been mitigated by the knowledge that the others were still safe and physically nearby.

I hadn't been brave enough to ask him. Perhaps I didn't feel as though I had the right.

Leona's bonds with the others had remained intact, of course—but I got the impression she would never be fully happy unless Kam was also part of that connection. At least Jax had probably been correct that Kam's connection would reappear whenever Leona was in heat. We just had to keep everybody alive that long.

Minsk was supposed to be a test run. Outside of Nikolayev's stomping grounds near St. Petersburg, the Eastern Bloc was likely to be the closest thing to friendly territory that we'd find. The underground had a network of sympathizers already embedded in the power structure in this part of the world. Additionally, many of those in power who weren't already sympathizers might be persuaded to join our cause with the lure of gaining prestige and prominence in a new post-Committee world order.

The trick would be extending our network of sympathizers into Western Europe, and eventually, the UFNA. If those two global superpowers turned our way, the rest of the world would follow. The Committee was a relatively weak presence in Africa, South America, and Australia to start with. Meanwhile, Asia's policy was usually heavily tied to its trading partners'.

The jet touched down in a jolt of squealing tires, the engines whining as they labored to slow the plane. A couple of turnings onto smaller taxiways, and the aircraft rolled to a stop next to a collection of sleek black vehicles that included a stretch limo. I'd have bet money that the cars were heavily armored and the glass bulletproof.

"Come. Commissariat Polonsky has arranged for our security escort to the hotel," Nikolayev said, leading the way as we deplaned and entered the limo.

Rhys Beckett had nearly burst an aneurysm when he found out that we'd be relying on outside security during this conference. I'd thought for a minute that we'd be scraping Nikolayev's innards off the ceiling of the sick room. Beckett wasn't someone whose bad side I'd ever wanted to get on, but an angry Beckett during late-term pregnancy was fucking terri-fying.

The fact that he was stuck on bed rest and unable to accompany us had led to a closed-door argument with Nikolayev—one that had risen to a truly impressive volume of yelling.

The interior of the limo was dark and elegant. Frankly I would have been more comfortable riding with the armed guards at the front of the convoy than sitting across from this pair of glittering omegas who'd practically begged me to make them mine. No one said much as the vehicles rolled out, heading for central Minsk. Flynn and Jax were in guard-dog mode. Nikolayev spent the journey looking out of the window as the convoy entered the city. Leona and Kam appeared completely absorbed in a folder of handwritten notes.

The Hotel Europa was old, expensive, and an intriguing mix of classical and modern. It had completely escaped the brutalist and constructivist architectural crazes that had struck this part of the world in the middle of the century. We stopped there only long enough to drop off our luggage—not even bothering to sweep for bugs yet, since we wouldn't be in the rooms for the next several hours anyway.

If the staff had any issues with extending service to two omegas and their alpha mates sharing one massive suite, they kept it to themselves. I placed my single suitcase in my single room, and tried to ignore the burn of acid in my throat at the knowledge that I could be in there with them. It would only take a handful of words.

Please, I want in.

I don't want to be alone.

Words I must never speak. Someone in this pack needed a clear head, because things were about to get dangerous. That someone was me. Despite the odds against us, I was determined that the others would never know what it felt like to lose a mate forever.

In no time at all, we reconvened in the hotel hallway and returned to the cars, heading for Independence Square, located a few blocks away. After some discussion, the decision had been made to hold this informal conference inside the so-called Government House, seat of the Belarusian unicameral parliament. We could have gone smaller—rented someplace private, or even used the nearby university—but Nikolayev didn't want 'small.' Nikolayev wanted the world's eyeballs on us.

The massive administrative building sat behind a twenty-foot-tall statue of Vladimir Lenin. It was composed of acres of elegant white stone, glass, and sharp right angles that reached unapologetically for the sky. Its aggressive modernity squared off with the classical architecture of the church and government buildings on the opposite side of the huge plaza. Everything here was designed to overwhelm the individual with its sheer scale.

The state is bigger than you, it said. *You don't stand a chance, little citizen.*

There was press waiting for us—unusual in this part of the world, to say the least. I sensed Nikolayev's hand in their presence, or possibly Polonsky's. Immediately, my instincts were on edge. More people meant more potential aggressors. Camera equipment and microphones meant it would be harder to spot hidden weapons. I sensed Jax and Flynn tensing as well.

All three of us were armed—heavily so. But we couldn't exactly open fire in a crowd full of journalists.

Across from me, Leona McCready straightened her shoulders and donned an aura of cool professionalism like a cloak. Kam's face was an unreadable mask; the same mask that had kept him from being discovered as an unregistered omega for nearly two decades spent in public life.

Unlike Leona, he might still pass as beta. The physical build. The beard. Both were thanks to testosterone injections, which he'd apparently continued during the months spent under Nikolayev's protection. But anyone with a nose would be able to tell that Leona was an omega. She'd been off pheromone suppressors since Cuba, presumably as a way to further torture me.

No one—betas included—could mistake the visceral punch behind that orange blossom and honey scent for artificial perfume.

Flynn, Jax, and I exited the limo, scoping out the crowd before parting to allow Nikolayev, Leona, and Kam out behind us. At Leona's appearance, the scrum of reporters burst into a confusion of Russian.

Nikolayev raised a quelling hand. "Questions in French and English only, please," he said.

"Is it true that the Committee intends to recognize equal rights for alphas and omegas?" asked a woman in heavily accented French.

"The Euro-Soviet branch now recognizes alphomic rights," Nikolayev replied. "The UFNA branch is still mired in decades of propaganda and corruption, under the leadership of the war criminal Enoch Sloane."

A male reporter shoved to the front. "You call Sloane a war criminal, yet you brutally murdered your own sister for being an omega?"

"Not true," Nikolayev said. "When she presented as an adolescent, my family and I faked her death in order to move her to an undisclosed location for her own safety."

"So she's still alive?" the man pressed. "That's quite a claim. Where is she? Can we speak with her?"

Nikolayev raised an eyebrow. "Perhaps you should investigate the definition of the word 'undisclosed.'"

"Isn't Leona McCready a wanted international fugitive?" called another journalist.

Leona stepped forward to speak for herself. I felt Jax and Flynn tense, their hard eyes raking the assembled group for threats.

"I do not acknowledge the validity of so-called laws designed to violate the human rights of a marginalized group." Leona met the reporter's gaze, refusing to back down as she continued. "My parents risked jail to protect me from slavery or forced sterilization as a child. A few months ago, I was pulled from my bed at three a.m. by an armed SWAT team who broke down my door without offering any sort of identification, or presenting a warrant for my arrest. That isn't the rule of law. That's fascism."

Silence fell, broken only by the frantic scratch of pens against notepads.

"Where are your parents now?" someone asked. "Do you have contact with them?"

"My parents are deceased," Leona said without breaking expression—a blatant lie, but I couldn't blame her for holding that card close to her chest.

"We are due inside for meetings," Nikolayev said. "Good day."

He ushered us toward the statue of Lenin and the massive doors beyond, ignoring the overlapping babble of questions chasing us. It remained to be seen how the press would spin our presence here, but on the positive side, at least none of them had been undercover assassins with guns hidden in their camera bags.

The conference dragged on for days, boring and surprisingly free of drama. I'd been surprised to find that there were other alphas here, working as security for some of the attendees. Other than that, it was in many ways reminiscent of all the times our team had acted as security for one diplomat or another during overseas summits. Beckett's presence would have been reassuring, but so far it had been quiet duty.

I could only follow the parts of the debate that happened within my immediate vicinity, and then, only if the speakers were using French rather than rapid-fire Russian. The goal had been to gain commitments from as many officials as possible to introduce new laws related to alphomic rights into their various legislatures. As far as I could tell, roughly half of those present had agreed, or were at least receptive to further talks.

In other words, it was going to be a painful slog—unless Leona and Nikolayev managed to shake some big names free in Western Europe. And once again, thinking like that was the reason I was standing against the wall with a shoulder holster under my black suit jacket, rather than determining policy somewhere. When it came to saving alphas and omegas, I simply wasn't that patient.

Personally, I would have been more inclined to fuel up those Black Hawk helicopters

Nikolayev had somehow acquired in Cuba and go lob a few missiles at Sloane's house.

This was the third day we'd been here, and every day it grew just a little bit harder to wrench my attention away from Leona and Kameron as they worked the room. Yes, I was supposed to be watching them—but only in the sense of making sure none of the people around them posed a threat. Definitely not in the sense of ogling the way Kam's mouth curved when he offered someone a polite smile, or trying to catch a glimpse of the silvery bite scars at the juncture of Leona's neck and shoulder.

Shit.

A server passed, pausing to offer me a drink from his silver tray. I took one of the glasses and sipped at it mindlessly, needing something to both cool me down in the stuffy room and act as a distraction from my unwanted thoughts.

I nursed the clear sparkling water for a few minutes before tipping the rest of it back and returning the glass to another server's tray. It was growing late. I got the sense that things were winding down for the evening, and still without a satisfactory conclusion. There had been talk of extending the talks for one more day, but after that, we would leave.

Even this deep in Euro-Soviet territory, Nikolayev was unwilling to tempt Enoch Sloane or the Beta Liberation Front into attempting something rash. It was probably the right call. By all accounts, Sloane's frustration at his own impotence was spilling over into fits of temper and unhinged screaming at his staff. As for the BLF, there was almost no useful intelligence available about them, leaving the terrorist organization an unpredictable and potentially deadly threat—as Jax could attest firsthand.

Something crashed from across the room, setting my instincts alight. An unintentional growl rose in my throat as I methodically scanned the venue, trying to localize the source of the disturbance while also keeping watch for anyone who might be intending to use the noise as a distraction for something more sinister.

My earpiece crackled. *"Assailant near the north entrance to the hall,"* Jax reported. *"It's one of the alpha security grunts."*

I craned to see. A large figure near the door roared, throwing a clumsy roundhouse punch that didn't seem to be directed at anyone in particular. People scuttled away, opening a bubble of space around the crazed alpha.

"What the fuck?" That was Flynn in my ear.

I was already moving toward Leona and Kam when the source of Flynn's shock grew clear. A second alpha across the room snarled and pulled a gun, only to be immediately tackled by several of his fellows. A shot rang out, followed by a trickle of plaster dust falling from the ceiling where the bullet had impacted.

Flynn appeared, his body acting as a physical barrier between the omegas and the threats. My heartbeat thundered. Sudden rage filled me at the idea that he alone should get to gather the pair up and hustle them toward the south door. Goddamn it—I *wanted* those omegas. I was the pack leader. I was the stronger one. Those omegas should be mine. They *would* be mine.

My clit throbbed in its sheath as a wave of lust slammed over me. My jaw ached with the sudden urge to bite, to claim. Jax was approaching now with Nikolayev, both of them grim-faced and angry. I needed to act before I was outnumbered. Boiling rage flooded my veins as I reached into my jacket, my fingers closing around the grip of my weapon.

I drew the Makarov and aimed it at my rival. Flynn's eyes fell on me and widened.

Flynn's eyes.

Flynn.

With a gasp, I flung the handgun away as if it had suddenly become red hot, staggering backward. With a shaking hand, I pressed a finger to my earpiece.

"I'm compromised," I croaked. "You need to subdue me before I lose control like the others.

My hip impacted the edge of a table, stopping my backward momentum and sending a half-empty punchbowl and trays of glasses dancing. I saw Flynn exchange a wide-eyed look with Jax, before they both converged on me.

As two rivals charged me, my hindbrain rose up and swallowed my rational awareness. I screamed in rage and sprang at them, ready to snap necks and claw out eyeballs. My nails raked dark skin, just missing my assailant's left eye. The second alpha took advantage of my failed attack and dodged right. Before I could block his swing, something heavy and solid slammed into my temple.

The impact rang through my skull, sending me crashing to my knees. A second blow followed before I could straighten. The darkness swirling at the edge of my vision rushed inward, chasing me into the black.

ELEVEN

Leona

KAM AND I clutched each other in shock as Alex drew a gun on Flynn, only to gasp as if in pain and throw it away a moment later. She staggered backward, saying something I couldn't make out over the shouts and screams of the panicking crowd. Another gunshot shattered the air behind us, and I flinched, trying to stay low.

Flynn had been attempting to shelter us with his body. With a sharp curse, he sprang toward his pack leader. A familiar blond form rushed past us at almost the same instant, yelling at us to take cover. Jax converged on Alex just as she lunged for Flynn, attacking him viciously. Through the bond, I could feel my mates' utter, confused horror at what was happening.

Before I could react, a tall form grabbed me by the shoulder and bore me down, forcing me roughly to my hands and knees between two tables. Kam landed next to me with a pained grunt. For the barest of moments, I was thrown back to the raid at my apartment—strong hands shoving me to the floor. But then

Nikolayev appeared, crouching in front of us—watching the room with a tactical eye.

"Can I assume that your female alpha hasn't turned traitor voluntarily?" he asked, with acid in his tone.

"Of course she hasn't," Kam snapped, evidently forgetting his bone-deep fear of the Russian alpha in the face of the implied accusation against Alex's character.

Before Nikolayev could respond, Jax appeared with Alex's unconscious form slung over his shoulders. Flynn was with him, a hand on Jax's arm as they scanned the room for imminent threats. Four jagged lines of blood ran down the side of Flynn's face.

"What the hell is going on?" I demanded, my voice emerging high-pitched and panicky.

"We need to get out," Flynn said.

"Alex said something about being compromised," Jax put in. "That's all we know."

"Drugs," Nikolayev muttered. "Did she drink anything? Eat anything?"

"No idea," Flynn said. "Not really the most pressing problem right now. South door's clear. *Move.*"

Nikolayev pulled Kam and me to our feet, backing off without comment when Flynn snarled and moved in to replace him as our bodyguard. Kam grabbed my hand and we made for the stream of people hurrying toward the double doors. No more gunshots sounded from behind us, so hopefully the armed alpha had been restrained.

I cursed the impractical stiletto heels I'd chosen in an attempt to give myself an impression of added height and authority. Flynn's alpha bristling kept us from being jostled too badly by the crowd, but there was still a growing crush of people at the bottleneck formed by the doorway.

My mind spun, trying to make sense of what had just happened. *Drugged*, Nikolayev had said. A drug that made alphas act crazy?

"This feels like sabotage—something that anti-alphomic interests can use as propaganda," Kam said, as we squeezed through the door and into the grand hallway beyond. "*Dangerous alphas disrupting a meeting of bleeding-heart betas who were only trying to help them*—that kind of thing."

"If Alex and the others were drugged, someone needs to round up the staff and servers so they can be questioned." Jax's strain was barely audible in his voice, but clear as day through the bond.

"Yes," Nikolayev said through gritted teeth. "They certainly do."

More security guards jogged toward us from elsewhere in the building, all of them armed with automatic weapons. I recognized Dzimitry Polonsky hurrying toward them with his hand raised.

"No weapons, please! I believe the situation is under control now," the Commissariat called out.

Nikolayev left to join him, shouting something about making sure the service entrances were locked down. Flynn urged us over to an empty stretch of wall and stood in front of us protectively. Kam immediately moved to check Alex's pulse and pupillary reaction as she hung limp in Jax's grip.

"We need to get her proper medical help," I said, when Kam gave me a nod indicating she didn't seem to be in immediate danger. "Do we have any idea what kind of drug this might have been? Something psychotropic, maybe?"

"I can tell you this much," Jax said grimly. "Her clit's poking me in the shoulder like a steel rod."

"She didn't just start attacking people around her randomly," Flynn said, not sounding any happier about things than Jax was. "She aimed that gun straight at my head."

"And you were protecting Leo and Kam at the time," Jax finished. "She looked at you and saw a sexual rival for omegas she wants."

"Maybe, yeah." Flynn prodded gingerly at the livid scratch marks on his face.

"You're saying someone gave these alphas some kind of substance that forced them into a rut?" Kam asked, looking ill.

Jax opened his mouth, but closed it without saying anything and clamped his jaw in frustration instead.

"Did either of you drink or eat anything?" I asked.

"No," Jax said. Flynn shook his head, indicating that he hadn't, either.

Nikolayev returned and ran an assessing gaze over us. "We're leaving. For the moment, the security forces believe your alpha was injured during the confusion—but if other officials dispute that and say she was waving a gun around, things could become complicated."

"She needs medical assistance," I said, my gaze heated as I pinned the Russian alpha's.

"No doubt she does." Nikolayev didn't back down. "And I would prefer she get it from doctors I trust, in a setting I can control. Not in the same city that just orchestrated a rather neat plot to undermine seven months' worth of our plans. We can be back at my family's private airstrip in Russia in two-and-a-half hours if we hurry."

I felt Jax and Flynn's ambivalence echoing through my thoughts. I shared it. Nikolayev was right about the risks involved in trying to get Alex help in Minsk. Yet none of us were happy with the idea of dumping her on a plane in her current condition and hoping for the best.

"She's tough," Kam said quietly. "But we'll need to restrain her during the flight, in case she regains consciousness and tries to attack again."

I didn't have a decent argument against the bald statement, and apparently neither did Flynn or Jax.

"Yes. Come," Nikolayev said. "We will return to a place of safety and assess the impact of this debacle from there."

He flagged down Commissariat Polonsky, who escorted us back to the waiting limo, using his influence to smooth the way past various hastily erected checkpoints inside the building. The crowd of journalists outside was conspicuous by its absence as we left, and I wondered who'd been responsible for that.

It was approaching nine p.m. local time—fully dark outside except for Minsk's glittering city lights.

"We'll drive directly to the airport," Nikolayev said, his tone clipped. "The Commissariat will see that our belongings are sent on from the hotel."

I spared a thought for whoever ended up with the job of packing and shipping Flynn's sex toys. Jax manhandled Alex's limp body into the back of the limo, before he and Flynn squeezed in as well, flanking her. Nikolayev wisely decided to ride in one of the other vehicles rather than risk being in an enclosed space with Alex, on the off chance that she woke up during the trip to the airport at the edge of the city.

His gray eyes landed on me before I could enter the limo with the alphas. "You and Mr. Patel should take one of the other cars as well."

I opened my mouth to argue, but Kam touched my wrist. "He's right. If she's in a chemically induced rut, our presence will only make things worse by rousing her territorial instincts."

My jaw clenched. I hated this. *Hated it.*

"We'll watch over her," Flynn said from the plush leather seat. "Let's just get where we're going so she can get some proper help, yeah?"

"Yeah," I whispered, and turned on my impractical heels—stalking toward the car parked behind the limo. Kam was right behind me, slipping into the back seat as well. I followed the mating bond inward, knowing that if anything alarming happened during the drive, I'd be able to tell.

"What a disaster," Kam said with a heavy sigh, as the convoy headed out. His head fell back, his eyes trained on the sedan's burgundy headliner. "If anyone was seriously hurt or killed back there, it'll make prime paranoia fodder for the bigots."

I closed my eyes for a moment in an attempt to center my thoughts, breathing in and out slowly. "Only if it gets out," I said eventually. "And if we can get ahead of it with the real narrative—that someone is intent on drugging and poisoning innocent people— maybe it will work in our favor."

Kam rolled his head from side to side to ease the muscles of his neck, his vertebrae popping audibly. "So, who do you think it was? The Beta Liberation Front? Or Sloane?"

"Or maybe both, since there's some evidence the BLF already has connections to the

UFNA branch of the Committee," I offered listlessly. As far as we'd been able to determine, that connection was the only conceivable way the authorities in Montreal could have discovered I was an unregistered omega. No one had known except for a handful of BLF terrorists who'd escaped the cave in Romania when Kam, Jax, and I had been rescued.

"Or it could be someone else that we don't even know about yet." Kam thumped the back of his skull lightly against the rear headrest.

"Possibly," I said, not in any hurry to entertain that particular prospect. "Let's worry about Alex now, and leave the rest of it for later."

"Agreed," Kam said. "Leo, we need to be thinking about how far we're willing to go to help her through this, if she doesn't snap out of it naturally."

I knew exactly what he was implying, but I had no desire to discuss the details in the presence of our car's driver and the stoic security guy riding in the passenger seat. I nodded instead, acknowledging that we would have that conversation as soon as we could do so privately.

If Alex had genuinely been thrown into a rut, it would be no different than when I'd gone into heat while trapped in that Romanian terrorist cell. Jax and Kam had helped me then. Kam and I were the most logical options to help Alex now—or at least, we would be once we got someplace physically safe.

Rut for alphas wasn't a biological imperative like heat was for omegas. Everything I'd been able to find on the subject implied that it was a holdover from earlier times—an evolutionary trait that was slowly on its way out. The idea of someone weaponizing an alpha's mating frenzy sparked a slow-burning rage in my chest.

Knowing that Jax and Flynn would be able to feel the emotion, I tamped it down as best I could. It wasn't that I didn't think they'd understand why I was so upset, but they didn't need the extra distraction right now. I only hoped Alex didn't wake up during the trip. Alpha skulls were hard, and alphas healed fast—but it would be best for everyone involved if Flynn and Jax didn't have to clock Alex again to keep her out cold.

The ride continued in silence, broken only by occasional exchanges in Russian over a walkie-talkie in the front seat. We arrived at the small airport to find very little activity. The convoy of vehicles pulled up to a hangar and parked outside after another exchange over the two-way radio.

The security guy craned around to look at us from the front seat. "The boss says stay here until the female alpha is safely restrained on the aircraft," he said, in heavily Russian-accented French.

Kam nodded acknowledgement, wrapping his fingers tightly around mine when I brushed fingertips against his hand. This whole thing was getting way too reminiscent of the *first* occasion Kam and I had been passengers on a plane belonging to Kostya Nikolayev.

"Things worked out surprisingly well the last time we did this," Kam murmured, effortlessly interpreting my thoughts without the need for an active mate-bond.

I squeezed his hand and gave a single nod. "Guess so."

Unfortunately, I didn't see any obvious way that this mess could result in a happy ending for anyone involved. Poor Alex. How she'd hate this.

Time dragged. According to Kameron's watch, it was only about twenty minutes until the radio crackled to life again, and the security guy waved us out of the vehicle. It felt like an eternity.

We cautiously boarded the plane. I was unsure what to expect, but the sight of Alex cuffed hand and foot to one of the airplane seats stopped me cold. It was exactly how Nikolayev's troops had restrained Jax during the flight to Cuba. Jax—currently seated in the row behind Alex—must have felt my pulse of alarm. He sent comfort through the link, catching my eyes in his summer-blue gaze.

"This was a pretty damned effective means of restraint, as much as I hate to say it," he said. "It's only for a couple of hours, and then we'll get her the help she needs."

I forced my body back into motion and took a seat, sitting two rows in front of Alex. Kam slipped in beside me. Nikolayev was already seated at the front of the plane, along with the handful of support staff that had accompanied us to the conference.

The preflight checks dragged every bit as badly as the wait in the car, but eventually we taxied onto the runway and took off, the acceleration pressing me against the seatback. Complete darkness lay beyond the small window until the small jet banked, revealing the twinkling lights of Minsk far below. The aircraft leveled out, and we were on our way back to safety.

Ninety minutes, I thought. *Please, Alex — just stay unconscious for another ninety minutes until we land.*

TWELVE

Kameron

ALEX STAYED unconscious for slightly less than thirty minutes—and then the screaming started. Not screams of fright, but screams of rage, interspersed with feral growling. There was *so much fury* in those sounds... a banshee railing against the unfairness of the world.

Leo sat stiff and unmoving in the seat next to me. I know that she was fighting the same gut-deep need that I was—the need to go to Alex and comfort an alpha in distress. An alpha we both desperately cared for.

Flynn, seated in the row behind us and in front of Alex, must have felt the urge through his bond with Leo. He reached around the seatback to grasp her shoulder. "Don't. It won't help. You two need to know that if you get within range of her teeth, she'll bite you. If she somehow got free of her restraints, she'd try to rape you. There's not a single thought in her head right now except *get to the omegas.*"

It wouldn't be rape, I thought, and I sensed Leo clenching her jaw to hold back similar words. This wasn't a discussion I was willing to have in front of Nikolayev and the gaggle of terrified support staff, but we *would* be having it once we landed.

Leo craned around the edge of the seat, and Alex's wild green gaze locked on her. The alpha lunged, getting her upper body partway into Flynn's row before the metal around her wrists pulled her up short. Spittle flew as she snapped at the air.

"*Fuck!*" Flynn ducked out of range, and Alex fell back, panting and snarling.

The flight was horrible. Alex's shrieks of frustrated anger grew hoarse with exhaustion as time went on. The metal frame of the seat creaked and clattered as she jerked against her restraints convulsively. I wanted to find whoever had done this to her, so I could watch Jax and Flynn beat them within an inch of their worthless, miserable lives.

By the time the plane descended toward the runway at Nikolayev's secure compound, it was after midnight. The Russian had remained stoic as a marble statue throughout the tortuous journey—but as we shed altitude, he stood and made his way to the cockpit.

He returned after only a couple of minutes and sat down again, pulling his seatbelt across his lap. "I've instructed the pilot to radio ahead and ensure medical staff are waiting with an appropriate dose of tranquilizer," he said, pitching his voice to be heard over Alex's wails of distress.

Alex lunged again, only to crash shoulder-first into the bulkhead when the plane banked for its final descent. I faced forward and closed my eyes, gripping my seat arms in an attempt to block out her obvious torment. It must have been windy outside, because the landing was rough, setting my already nauseated stomach roiling.

After an endless few minutes, the plane rolled to a stop, its engines powering down with a whine. The cabin's low lights brightened, turning everything gleaming and white. The unfortunate staff members who'd been stuck on this flight from hell wasted no time in disembarking. They were replaced almost immediately by the doctor who'd been attending Beckett during his pregnancy, along with a burly man dressed as an orderly.

"You believe she was drugged?" the doctor asked.

"That's the current theory," Nikolayev replied tightly. "An unknown substance delivered orally via food or drink to induce a state of alpha rut."

'Well, *fuck*," said the doctor. "That's all the world needs right now. We'll definitely have to sedate her in order to remove her from the plane safely."

He gestured Jax and Flynn to vacate their seats in front of and behind Alex. Setting his medical bag on an empty seat nearby, he withdrew a pre-loaded hypodermic needle and tapped it to release the air bubbles. "She's probably close to exhaustion by now. Vasiliev, restrain her from behind long enough for me to get this into her arm."

I watched with deep misgivings as Vasiliev headed for her. Alex roared and jerked against the cuffs with her full strength. With a sharp, metallic crack, the welds on the seat arm gave way. She took a wild swing at the orderly, the angled hunk of metal arcing out like a weapon, still attached to the other end of the handcuff. Vasiliev cursed and stumbled backward, the heavy length missing his head by barely an inch.

"What the hell is going on in here?" A familiar voice, breathless with exertion, echoed from just outside the cabin door. In our relatively short acquaintance, I'd come to associate that voice with safety and stability. Rhys Beckett stormed onto the plane, one hand wrapped protectively over his swollen belly and his pale eyes snapping fire.

Nikolayev was halfway to him before I could so much as blink. *"Solnishko,* you should not be out of bed!"

"If you wanted me to stay in my fucking bed, you should have done a better job of dampening your worry through the bond." Beckett's growl was worthy of any alpha. "Jax—report, damn it!"

Jax practically snapped to attention beneath the whip-crack order. "She's in full rut, sir. The doctor wants to sedate her so we can move her, but we can't get close to restrain her."

Beckett's gaze raked over the small collection of people left in the cabin. "Everyone get off the plane. Doctor, give me the sedative." His attention fell on me, assessing. "Kam, you've got no pheromones to rile her up. You can stay."

Nikolayev straightened to his full height. "This isn't safe for you. The pregnancy—"

Beckett's lips pulled back in a silent snarl of warning. "*Get. Off. The damned. Plane.*"

Nikolayev took an involuntary step backward. Apparently, no one had warned him about trying to steamroll a pregnant omega.

Beckett softened almost imperceptibly. "I already have pups, Kostya. You know that. And one of them needs me right now."

As if to punctuate the statement, Alex shrieked again. The broken chair arm flew through the air and cracked sharply against the tiny airplane window, still attached to the handcuff chain.

Nikolayev stared Beckett down for a long moment before giving a single, sharp nod. "Do as he says."

Leo gave me a pleading look as I rose to let her squeeze past me into the aisle. "Be careful, odama."

I pressed a kiss to her temple. "Always. We'll figure out what to do next, just as soon as she's someplace safe."

Jax and Flynn followed Leo toward the cabin door, each of them resting a hand on my shoulder as they shuffled past me in a brief gesture of support. I doubt they would have willingly left Alex alone on anyone else's orders, but one word from Beckett was all it took.

The doctor handed over the loaded syringe to his pregnant patient. He didn't look pleased, but there was resignation in his tone when he said, "I'll be waiting outside. You already know this is ill-advised, yes?"

"I've made a successful career out of doing things that are ill-advised," Beckett replied. "I'll send Kameron out to inform you once she's safely out cold."

The man shook his head ruefully, but he didn't argue. With a sharp gesture to his assistant, he led the way to the exit. Once we were alone with Alex, Beckett's tense shoulders slumped. A heartbeat later, he grunted and curled forward, his teeth gritted as he clutched at his distended abdomen for a long moment before straightening cautiously.

A sinking sensation took up residence in my gut. "You're going to bring on your labor prematurely," I said.

He took a couple of deep breaths and let his hand fall to his side. "Can't be helped. And I'm only a couple weeks out from my due date." He indicated Alex, whose violent outburst had subsided into low growls. "The faster we get her the support she needs, the faster I can get back in that blasted, ridiculous bed."

I nodded. "You think your pregnancy pheromones will calm her?"

It was unclear if that was what had halted Alex's rampage, or if it was merely the fact that almost everyone had left the cabin.

"It should help." Beckett quickly checked the syringe. "Alphas tend to get very protective around pregnant omegas. Stay back until I call for you. I'm guessing you know your way around a needle from testosterone injections, yes?"

"As long as it's intramuscular, I can do it," I said.

"Good." He handed me the syringe. "I'll hold her and try to keep her calm. When I tell you it's safe, come stand in the row behind her and inject her in the shoulder. Watch out for that loose seat arm."

"All right," I said. "But for the love of god, try not to get brained, bitten, or otherwise damaged. Your mate would wring my neck with his bare hands."

"Actually, he's partial to firing squads," Beckett replied. "Stay here."

I stared after him. It was probably meant as a joke.

Probably.

Alex sat hunched in her broken seat, panting rapidly. Her curtain of dark hair obscured her expression, but low snarls still emerged from her lips every few seconds. Beckett approached her slowly, his posture open. *Look at me*, it said. *I'm totally harmless. Just a defenseless pregnant omega, no threat to you at all.*

In Beckett's case, that body language was deeply misleading — but it worked well enough to keep Alex from erupting into fresh violence as he moved closer.

"*Alex*," he said — a beloved carrier soothing a distraught pup.

My throat tightened, long-buried memories of family and loving arms holding me bubbling to the surface. Alex peeked out from the shelter of her hair. She snarled again, baring her teeth, but the sound choked off in a whimper. I held my breath as Beckett closed the final distance separating them, half-expecting the metal seat arm to go flying toward his head.

It didn't, although it did clatter as she raised her freed hand, reaching for him. A terrible, keening moan rose from her throat — the weak cry of an injured animal caught in a trap. Beckett angled his unwieldy belly into the cramped space in front of her and let her clutch at him.

"All right," he said, wrapping an arm around her heaving shoulders and placing a steadying hand on the nape of her neck. "We've got you now. You're going to be okay, you hear me? Kam's here, too. He's going to give you a shot in your left shoulder that will make you sleep. And when you wake up, things will be better."

Beckett met my eyes and gave a beckoning jerk of his chin.

"We're all safe now," I said, approaching with the same unthreatening omega body language Beckett had used. "We're back at Nikolayev's compound, so it's fine to rest for a bit. Everything's okay, but I do need to give you this injection. I'd say something about a little prick, but that would be crass since there are two male omegas present."

Beckett snorted in dark amusement.

I slipped into the space behind Alex's seat, giving the syringe a final check and popping the protective cap off the needle. "Don't laugh. You probably haven't seen your own prick in months, Mr. Preggo," I said, and slid the needle in, depressing the plunger.

I'd been on high alert, prepared to duck an attack and praying Beckett could also move quickly if he needed to. Alex only jerked — letting out a low warning growl, but not moving from his protective hold.

"There, now," he said, stroking her hair. "Let's give that a minute or two to kick in, shall we?"

I capped the spent needle and moved into the aisle, ready to retreat again. To my surprise, Alex reached for me with her freed arm, her fingers outstretched and grasping. Caught out, I sent Beckett a questioning look. He nodded. After setting the syringe safely out of the way, I took Alex's hand and pressed it between both of mine.

Her wrist was horribly bruised from the cuff, and the broken seat arm clanked against the chair frame as we stood there in the deserted private jet—me in the aisle, and Beckett still jammed awkwardly into the gap between seat rows. Alex rocked restlessly in our grips, her body quieting by gradual degrees until a long sigh escaped her lungs and she slumped forward.

Beckett, looking decidedly pasty, eased her back and half-collapsed into the seat next to her. His jaw clenched, and his arm returned to clutch at his belly.

"We need to discuss what will happen if I'm not in a position to stay with her until she's better," he said tightly.

And… *balls*. I'd been right. He was going into labor.

"I haven't spoken with Leo yet, but I'm open to helping Alex with this," I said, ignoring the elephant-sized baby belly in the room—at least for now.

Beckett looked up at me. Sweat beaded his brow. "And you understand what that will mean? Truly?"

"Yes," I said.

His pain-filled gaze didn't let up. "She'll try to bite you. But in her right mind, she wouldn't want that."

"I know," I snapped. It wasn't as though the implications had escaped me. All I'd have to do was get my neck near Alex's teeth, and I'd have that third mating bite I'd craved so badly. All it would take was compromising my morals and taking advantage of a helpless sex partner trapped in a chemical rut.

"Right. Of course you do." Beckett sounded apologetic. "God, what a fucking mess."

He went suddenly very still, and looked down at his lap. I followed his gaze to find his loose cotton pajama pants soaked along the inner thighs. The smell of blood hit me an instant later. The fabric was tinged red where his water had broken.

"Damn and blast," Beckett said. "I suppose you'd better go and get the doctor in here now."

THIRTEEN

Leona

I STOOD BETWEEN Jax and Flynn's reassuring bulk, feeling the minutes tick by like molasses as Beckett and Kam did whatever they were doing to try and calm Alex enough to sedate her. Not for the first time, I was struck by the alphas' unyielding faith in Beckett's ability to fix any given situation, no matter how badly screwed up it was.

Tension crackled off Nikolayev in waves, as he, too, awaited word. Unlike us, he had a direct line to whatever was happening inside the plane via his mating bond. As it did at odd moments, the utter unfairness of Kam's situation hit me. We were bonded, but not really. Not when it counted.

Flynn put his arm around my shoulders and stroked me, soothing.

"They'll take care of it," Jax said. "Don't worry."

Nikolayev stiffened. A moment later, his chest rumbled with a warning growl and he headed for the metal steps leading to the door of the aircraft. My anxiety spiked.

He was halfway up when Kam appeared in the doorway. "Alex is down for the count, but Beckett's water just broke," he called down. "Doctor, we need you in here."

Nikolayev broke into a run, taking the steps three at a time. Kam's eyes widened in alarm, and he ducked out of the way just in time to avoid being bowled over.

"You gonna need help, doc?" Jax asked. "You've only got one gurney."

The grim-faced doctor eyed the rolling cot. "Yes. Assuming she's otherwise uninjured, if one of you can carry your alpha, we'll put Mr. Beckett on the gurney. I should warn you, if this is a true rut, there's not really much to be done for your pack member beyond the obvious."

I had a pretty good idea of what was meant by 'the obvious.' We'd be facing that topic soon enough—but it needed to be a decision we made together.

Flynn followed the doctor and his orderly onto the plane. Once the way was clear, Kam jogged down to join us on the ground. Probably a good thing, since the last thing the others needed was more people underfoot inside the cramped interior of the jet.

"Alex calmed down enough that we were able to sedate her without anyone getting hurt," Kam said quietly. "But Beckett's labor just started two weeks early, and he's bleeding."

"Oh, no," I whispered. All the talk of his pregnancy being high-risk had been yet another background worry in my mind, but I'd mostly managed to avoid thinking about the reality of the danger to him and his unborn pup. The idea that he might be bleeding out from a ruptured placenta less than a hundred feet away from us made bile rise in my throat.

"At least there's qualified medical staff here," Kam offered.

Nikolayev appeared with Beckett in his arms. Both of their faces were gray with strain. I held my breath as the pair descended the narrow rolling staircase, but Nikolayev never missed his footing. He made a beeline for the gurney and laid his mate on it. Beckett had rushed to the plane in the clothing he'd been wearing while on bed-rest. The thin pajama pants were soaked with clear fluid and tinged with blood, but thankfully not stained bright scarlet.

Please let him be okay, I sent to any deity that might be listening. *Please let the pup be alive.*

Flynn followed with Alex in his arms. The metal cuffs still hung from her wrists and ankles. I had a nasty feeling this was because we might need to restrain her again when we got her to wherever we were going. In no time, the nine of us were heading for the main house—the orderly pushing the gurney at a brisk pace while the doctor jogged alongside, checking Beckett's pulse and blood pressure.

It wasn't a short trek to get to the main house, but it wouldn't have saved much time to try and use a car. Considering the difficulty of moving the patients in and out of a vehicle, it made sense to travel on foot, making use of the concrete walkways wending around the property. When we finally arrived at the palatial house, the doctor helped the orderly get the gurney up the low steps leading to the massive front doors.

Inside, he led the way to a large elevator, and we descended to the basement level. It was the first time I'd had cause to come down here, but it came as little surprise that Nikolayev had a pretty decent medical clinic tucked away inside his massive family home. I wondered if Irina had recovered in one of these small, white rooms after Nikolayev had rescued her from the UFNA branch of the Committee.

Nikolayev and the doctor disappeared into one room with Beckett. The orderly gestured Flynn to bring Alex into another and put her on the bed, where he immediately fastened the handcuffs to the metal bed frame. Jax, Kam, and I huddled outside the door, not wanting to be in the way given the room's limited space.

"The physician will be in to take her vitals and draw blood as soon as he can," the orderly—Vasiliev—told us. "Like he said before, there's probably not much to be done medically. You, uh, might want to talk about other options, if that's on the table. If you need help, we're next door."

He checked Alex's cuffs to make sure they were secure, and then squeezed past us with a nod before disappearing into Beckett's room. Once he was gone, I exchanged looks with Kam and Jax. We joined Flynn inside the modest room, and Jax closed the door behind us. Kam moved to take Alex's cuffed wrist in his hand, his fingers on her pulse point. With his other hand, he peeled back her eyelids to check her pupils.

I understood that Beckett's condition was more of an emergency right now, and I didn't begrudge him the doctor's attention—but it did feel like Alex was something of an afterthought at the moment.

"Time for real talk," Jax said.

Kam nodded. "Beckett was able to calm her down—probably due to his pregnancy pheromones. Unfortunately, he's not in a position to help now. I know this is complicated by the fact that the four of us are mated and she isn't part of that, but I intend to help her if there's nothing the doctor can do medically to interrupt the rut."

Flynn shifted uncomfortably in place. "It's complicated, all right. Alex is still pack, though—even if she won't admit it to herself. But, Ginger Tea, you've only got one place for that knot to go... and it's not a place that's gonna stand up well to an alpha in full rut. She'll tear you up bad."

"We'll tag team her," I said without hesitation. "I can try to take the brunt of it. Does anyone here know how long this is likely to last?"

Please, let it not be days on end, like an omega heat.

There was a longish silence, broken only by Alex's ragged breathing from the bed.

"I'm not sure we can predict it with any accuracy, since it's not a natural rut," Kam said eventually. "And honestly, these days ruts are more of an urban legend than anything else."

"I've only ever heard about them happening during the last day of a heat coupling," Jax said. "And to be fair, things *can* get pretty intense around that time."

"So, maybe a day or so, but we don't really know for sure," I summarized. "It's already been three hours, and the sedative will keep her under for a while. I mean… I don't suppose the doctor could just keep her sedated through the whole thing?"

That would almost certainly be the best option, at least for Alex's peace of mind afterward. I wasn't at all sure how she'd react to having been fucked without her consent—even by Kam and me.

Who was I kidding? *Especially* by Kam and me.

"You can't drug an omega through a heat," Kam said dully. "The required dose just keeps getting higher and higher, until eventually it would kill them to keep trying. This is probably similar."

Well, shit. I tried to recenter my brain around logistics rather than emotions. "We'll need a way to ensure she can't bite." I saw Kam's small flinch, quickly hidden. He'd clearly thought about that possibility already. "We might want to be mated to her," I said, more gently, "but she's made it clear she doesn't want to be mated to us. We have to make sure it can't happen accidentally."

"I've got something for that," Flynn said in a flat tone.

I didn't waste any time being incredulous over Flynn's vast stockpile of sex aids, opting instead for practicality. "You mean you've got something here? Not in our luggage in Belarus?"

"It's here," Flynn said, unrepentant as always when it came to his sex toy collection. "Got it for Kam in case he might like it, but it'll work for this, too."

"She'll need to be restrained the whole time, so she can't hurt you," Jax said, sounding like the idea made him sick. "You have to be able to get away from her if you need to."

"And we're going to be present, in case something happens and you need muscle." Flynn didn't make it seem like a negotiable point.

"Having other alphas in the room could enrage her," Kam said. He sounded every bit as queasy about the whole thing as Jax had.

"As opposed to how mellow and chill she's gonna be if we're not there?" Flynn asked pointedly.

"He's right," Jax said. "We won't bend on this one, you two. Alex is our pack, but she doesn't get to hurt you. Period."

A faint rumble of a growl sounded from the bed. We turned as one to look at Alex, but she subsided after a moment and lay unmoving.

"Sounds like we're not gonna have loads of time to iron out the details here," Flynn said unhappily.

Kam sighed. "I'll go and let the doctor know she's stirring. Hopefully he can leave Beckett long enough to at least run some basic tests on her."

He ducked out. Once the door swung closed behind him, Jax turned to look at me.

"He's thinking about taking advantage of Alex's condition to mate her," he said, keeping his tone even.

"Everyone in this room has thought about it," I shot back, a pulse of reproach escaping me to thrum through the bond. "And that doesn't mean any of us would actually act on it—Kam included."

The doctor bustled into the room, with Kam in his wake. He wasted no time undoing the top few buttons on Alex's rumpled white shirt and pressing a stethoscope to her chest. He checked her pupils as Kam had done, strapped a blood pressure cuff to her arm, and finally drew a vial of blood. When the needle slid into her vein, Alex whined and jerked weakly before subsiding again.

"I can't rule out a mild concussion from that bruise on her temple," the doctor said. "Her pulse and blood pressure are elevated, but that's to be expected. You understand there's not a whole lot I can do for her, and I've got an emergency on my hands in the other room."

He looked at the four of us, his expression grave. "If you can do so safely, and if everyone's willing, take her somewhere and keep her restrained so your omegas can help her through this without anyone getting hurt. If that's not an option, she'll just have to stay here under observation and tough it out. I'll monitor her for dangerously high blood pressure readings, but that's about all I can do."

"We'll help her," I said firmly, choosing to look past the 'your omegas' language.

"We can take her to the nest in the guesthouse," Flynn said. "Maybe that will help calm her down."

"How's Beckett doing?" Jax asked.

"His condition is precarious," said the doctor. "As is the pup's condition. I apologize if I seem dismissive of your alpha's situation. But frankly, I can be of much more use to my other patient right now than I can be to this one. I'll run the blood tests as quickly as I can, and if that yields anything useful I'll let you know."

"As long as it's only a rut, she'll live," Flynn said. "Although she probably won't enjoy it for the next little while."

"If we're moving her, let's go." Kam shot Alex a nervous look. "I just saw her hand twitch again."

"I think we can risk one more sedative shot," the doctor said. "It won't last as long as the first, but it will give you time to get her to your nest." He went to a small refrigerator in the corner of the room and retrieved a syringe and a vial, drawing up another dose of drugs and injecting Alex in the hip.

A cry of pain filtered through to us from the room next door.

The doctor straightened and sighed. "I must leave you now."

"We've got her from here." Flynn reached in his pocket and retrieved the key to the handcuffs.

"We'll call you if there are any problems we can't handle," Jax added. "Do your best for Beckett's pup, all right?"

The man nodded and left. I wondered if the others had truly realized that Beckett's own life was in danger—not just his pup's. I tamped the thought down before it could go further. We couldn't help Beckett right now. We *could* help Alex. I'd been where she was before—feeling my body betraying me and being unable to do anything about it. If Kam and I could help it, Alex wouldn't have to suffer in that terrible purgatory for long.

FOURTEEN

Alex

THERE WAS AN omega in the room. The scent of sweet orchards and honey penetrated the overwhelming haze that had weighed down my mind and body, shrouding me in burning darkness. My clit throbbed, pulsing with painful need.

But we weren't alone. *Rivals.* The heavy odor of other alphas sent my hindbrain galloping with the desire to fight, to kill, to *claim.* Spicy musk and mossy cedar filled my nose. Familiar, but still my enemies. They would stand between me and the omega… or, maybe there had been two omegas? I thought there had been two before.

It didn't matter. They would try to keep me from taking what should be mine, and I would have to kill or maim them to get what I wanted.

My body felt too heavy, like something was sitting on my chest. Like my arms and legs were pinned down. Alarm thrummed through my veins. If I couldn't kill the alphas first, they'd kill me and keep the omegas for themselves. The burst of adrenaline woke my nerves and lent fresh strength to my muscles.

"Alex?" The voice was soft. Female. Close. The scent of sweet orange blossoms smothered me. I tried to pounce and snap my teeth, the desire to bite and mark and fuck making my head spin.

There was something in my mouth. It tasted of rubber and I couldn't spit it out—a tough cylinder stretching my lips back like a bit and bridle strapped onto a horse. I couldn't bite through it or push it out with my tongue. I tried to reach up with my hands and rip it off, but I couldn't move my arms. Rope tugged at my wrists. I thrashed and snarled, the sound distorted and muffled around the rubber gag. My legs were trapped, too.

Animal panic flooded me. I had to get free... I couldn't be helpless when the alphas came to kill me. I shrieked and flailed, desperate to escape before rough hands closed around my throat to snap my neck and take the omegas away forever.

They couldn't, *they couldn't*! I had to breed... I had to put pups inside those omegas or the world would end!

"*Alex!*" A different voice—this one male and sounding near to tears, as I screamed through the gag and wrenched at the ropes. "Alex, please! You'll hurt yourself! We're here; we're going to help. Oh, Alex, I'm so sorry..."

Hands landed on me, but they were soft. Not the alphas, ready to kill me. If I was fast enough, if I could only get free, maybe I could still breed this one before the other alphas could stop me. The ache in my clit was growing unbearable.

"Alex." It was the female again. Gentle hands tugged at the closures of my pants. Fingers brushed against my erection, and I arched off the soft surface beneath me as though I'd been electrocuted.

"I've been where you are, okay?" the voice continued. "I know you don't need coddling and reassurance. You just need to be knotting us. But if you can understand me at all, I swear to you that things will be all right afterward. Nothing will change between us unless you want it to."

Fingers were tugging my slacks over my hips... pulling my underwear down enough to free my hard, hypersensitive clit.

"We're going to take turns with you," said the male voice. "We promise, we won't let you be without one or the other of us. You can probably smell the other alphas, but they're not going to stop us or hurt you."

That was bullshit. The alphas wouldn't let these perfect, delectable omegas mate someone else without a fight. *I* would fight. I'd punch and kick and claw and rip—

Honey and orange blossoms crawled on top of me, straddling my hips. I keened, arching up again, trying to push the omega where I needed her.

"Easy." The male omega's hand stroked my forehead, pushing my sweat-soaked hair away from my face. "We've got you, Alex. We've got you."

Slick folds dragged along my length, positioning me. I was already burning up, lava running through my veins, but sliding into the omega's passage was like falling into the sun. I sobbed, and snarled, and tried again to bite through the infuriating gag preventing me from getting my teeth into the female omega's flesh.

It wasn't enough. It could never be enough—but she rode me, and the male omega twined his fingers with mine. I grabbed hard and held, my nails digging into skin as my teeth longed to do. I would breed them, and breed them, and *breed* them, over and over until the other alphas stopped me. I would fill them full of my spunk and knot them so none of it could spill out. I would take them both; have them both, again and again until our pups took over the entire world.

My shirt was half undone at the top. The female made soothing, shushing noises over the sound of my growling and snarling. Her small hand delved inside the rumpled fabric, smoothing over my flat breast and thumbing the nipple. I snapped my hips into her with wild abandon, lifting her body with every violent thrust. She gasped and pinched the pebbled peak hard enough to hurt. The pulse of pain went straight to my clit, and just like that I was coming, coming—shooting inside her with spurt after agonizing spurt.

She groaned in the way that only a well-fucked omega can, her body clamping around me as my knot swelled, locking us together.

It should have been a relief, but it wasn't. Not remotely. The alphas were still here, and now I was even more helpless than before—locked with my mate, pinioned and unable to get free. I couldn't bite her and cement the mating bond. I had to guard the nest. I *couldn't* guard the nest. A whimper of distress escaped me. This was *terrible*.

Hands and voices soothed me… but they were lies. This was the end of the world. I hadn't even bred the other omega yet. My knot ached, pulsing in time with my frantic heartbeat. The female omega smelled distressed. I couldn't smell the male omega at all. I'd been right—something was wrong. *Everything* was wrong. This was wrong, and I was wrong, and I couldn't *fix* any of it because I couldn't *move*.

Tears of frustration trickled down my face, and I *hated* them. The only thing that was right was my seed trapped inside the omega's passage, and her muscles clamping around my knot like she wanted it there.

Minutes ticked by, marked by the thumping beat of my heart. Time marched endlessly, until finally her body released mine and my knot subsided. My erect clit didn't. I needed to fuck, and keep fucking, like doing so could somehow stave off the huge, horrible *something* hanging over my head.

The female slid off me with a groan, but before I could panic again, she curled up with her head on my shoulder. And then, the male was there. He was lithe and pretty and oddly familiar, but it drove me mad not to be able to scent him properly. I squirmed, trying to get lined up because he kept trying to put my clit in the wrong place. I couldn't get any leverage though, and he was insistent in his movements. With a hiss, he guided me inside him. It was tight, and hot, and satiny smooth, making me forget in a flood of sensation that I wouldn't be able to get him pregnant like this.

Instinct took over, and I thrust up, drawing a yelp from him.

"Kam?" It was an alpha voice, low and wary.

I growled my deepest warning growl, having momentarily forgotten about the other alphas who would try to stop me from having this omega. Frustration had me jerking fruitlessly at my bonds again.

"It's all right," said the omega, his voice tight and high-pitched. "Stay back, both of you. I'm all right."

He didn't sound all right. I jerked my hips into him sharply to make him forget whatever was bothering him, and he gasped.

"Easy. *Easy* now, Alex." The female murmured her words against the crook of my neck, but I didn't *want* easy. I wanted to fuck.

I chewed at the infuriating rubber in my mouth, my jaw muscles straining as I continued to drive into the male omega's ass. His soft hands splayed palm-down on my shoulders as he braced himself against my body and took the pounding I was giving him. The female's clever fingers returned to tease my nipples. When her little omega teeth nipped sharply at the tendon running down the side of my neck, I shouted and came again.

The male cried out in counterpoint, clenching. For the second time, I popped a knot inside a hot passage. I fell back, panting.

"Kam," the female said, her distressed pheromones choking the air around us. "Talk to us."

The male was shaking. "It's okay. I'm okay. She can't help being rough."

I didn't want him shaking like that. I wanted him sated and pregnant. I wanted him *claimed*. I gnashed my teeth furiously against the gag.

"Let one of the others check you out once she lets you go," said the female, her scent still sour with worry. "I want to make sure you're not bleeding."

"I will," the male replied. "Please try not to worry. She can smell it on you."

"Sorry," the female said, sounding contrite. Her scent moderated to something more neutral as the minutes passed, and I relaxed a bit.

I couldn't understand why the alphas weren't intervening. At first, I thought maybe they were also restrained like I was—but they didn't seem to be. No one in the room was happy, but as the hours dragged on, I always had an omega to fuck and knot. It was impossible not to let my guard down, at least a little.

It was the female riding me, mostly, but I still knotted the male three times. My clit felt like it was about to snap off at the root from overuse, but I couldn't stop. The world would implode if I stopped. The omegas grew ever more pliant and yielding as time passed, sprawling bonelessly over my body whenever we were tied together. The scent of distress gave way to a scent of exhaustion. I liked that better, even if it still wasn't right. I liked the way they felt when they trusted their weight to me, pressing me into the softness of the mattress at my back.

Maybe that part was almost as good as fucking. Maybe it would be okay to have the weight of drowsy omegas on me without having my clit buried deep inside them. As if the thought had flipped some kind of a switch inside my mind, darkness washed over me and I tumbled into sleep.

FIFTEEN

Alex

SOMEONE WAS STABBING an ice pick through my right eye. I tried to swallow and lick my lips. My jaw hurt. My tongue hurt. Not like I'd accidentally bitten it, though. More like I'd been using it to do dumbbell curls.

I was lying on a bed. The room was dim—soothingly lit with warm, reddish light. *A nest.* My head wasn't the only thing that hurt. My sheathed clit throbbed like someone had kicked me square between the legs with a steel-toed boot. My wrists and ankles felt bruised. The side of my neck was tender.

One of my idiot packmates was sitting in a chair beside the bed. Jax eyed me warily as I groaned and tried to roll into a sitting position, only to fall back on the bed in an ignominious heap.

"Good morning," he said. "What's the last thing you remember?"

There was no world in which a question phrased like that led to anything good. Against my better judgment, I cast my mind back.

"We were—" I began, only to descend into dry coughing.

Jax handed me a cup. I took it and drank, noting in a detached sort of way that my hand was trembling. A dribble of water trickled down my chin.

"We were… in Belarus?" I managed, handing the cup back.

Jax set it aside and returned to his chair. "Yes," he agreed. "At the conference."

The conference. We'd been there with Nikolayev and the omegas, meeting with Irina's mate—*husband*—and several other dignitaries from countries around the region. Things had been going decently well, if not spectacularly so. There'd been talk of extending the meetings for an additional day. I'd been watching Leona and Kam work, berating myself for letting them distract me from scanning for threats like I was supposed to be doing. And then—

I blinked.

Rage. Lust. Terror.

Bodies writhing against mine. Soft words that might as well have been gibberish. Reassurances that I couldn't allow myself to believe. I felt the blood drain from my face so quickly that it made me lightheaded.

"No…" I whispered.

"*Alex.*" Jax's voice cut through my growing panic. "Look at me, alef."

I dragged my gaze to his blue eyes, staring at him past a hazy memory of sighting along my gun barrel at Flynn's head.

"We're back in Russia," Jax said. "No one's injured. You didn't mate either of them.

They helped you of their own free will, with the full expectation that it wouldn't change anything afterward."

"I didn't bite them?" The words were a barely audible rasp.

"No one bit anyone." He paused, seeming to rethink the statement. "Correction. No one *mated* anyone. Actually, your neck is a mass of bruises, because apparently Leo has a not-so-secret marking fetish. She didn't break the skin, though."

My body flushed hot, then cold. "And she wasn't in heat." That was right, wasn't it? She hadn't been due for a heat... had she?

"No one's pregnant," Jax said firmly. "And no one's mated to you. Someone at the conference spiked the drinks with a drug that brings on a rut in alphas—probably one of the staff. You and two other alphas got dosed. Nikolayev's doctor ran blood tests on you, and he doesn't seem to think there will be any lasting effects."

"A drug. For alphas," I repeated stupidly, trying to get more neurons firing in sequence.

"If your first thought was *Beta Liberation Front*, so was ours." Jax took a deep breath and let it out in a huff. "It was probably meant as a way to get alphas to hurt or kill people, so the story could be spread over the worldwide news media to reinforce Enoch Sloane's message about the so-called alphomic menace."

I swallowed hard. "Did I..."

"No one at the conference was seriously injured. You pulled a gun on Flynn, but you threw it away an instant later when you realized you were compromised. One of the other alphas in the room got off a few shots, but he didn't hit anybody. I knocked you out. We bundled you onto Nikolayev's plane and brought you back here, where we're secure." He hesitated. "Sorry about pistol-whipping you like that, alef."

They'd kept me from hurting anyone. They'd brought me back. They'd let their precious omega mates fuck me through a rut, and made sure I couldn't bite them or hurt them too badly in the throes of my madness.

Jesus Christ.

"Leave," I said, because I was in danger of falling to pieces and I didn't want him here.

"There's something else," he told me, not rising from his chair. "Beckett whelped a female pup yesterday. It's been touch and go. He's still recovering. The pup's in an incubator, two weeks premature and pretty damned tiny. He'll want to see you as soon you're up to it."

Derailed, I took a moment to try and wrap my brain around that revelation. Nikolayev and Beckett had a daughter? Good god — she'd probably end up ruling the world when she grew up.

I shook my head to dislodge the non sequitur, and regretted it immediately when my eyeballs pulsed like they might roll right out of my skull. "I need to talk to Leona and Kameron," I muttered.

"They're resting at the moment," Jax said, in a carefully neutral tone. "You probably should be, too. I'll let them know you're awake and wanting to see them. I'll also have Flynn bring you something to eat."

My stomach protested the idea of food, but I hadn't eaten in who knew how long, so I nodded.

"Thank you." The words were harder to get out than they should have been.

Jax rose, looking down at me with a troubled expression. "Alex... this thing with Leo and Kam—we need to figure it out. They're dead set on not pressuring you into anything you don't want to do. But, me? I'm starting to worry about what will happen to our pack, long term."

I heard what he wasn't saying. If I'd had a mate-bond with the rest of them, I wouldn't have pulled a gun on Flynn, because I wouldn't have perceived him as a threat. Leo, as an omega, would have been able to soothe my emotions through the psychic link to keep me from losing my shit.

Basically, all of this could have been avoided. My stomach churned harder.

"I hear you, alef," I said. "I do."

He nodded, satisfied—at least for now. "We can talk more later. The doc didn't want to give you any painkillers until you woke up and we saw how you were doing, but there's aspirin on the table next to the water."

Leaning down, he gave my shoulder a squeeze before turning and leaving the room… leaving me alone with my whirling thoughts.

Everyone wanted me mated to Kam and Leona. I'd been helpless during the rut—a slave to my alpha hormones. All they would have needed to do was put a neck in range of my teeth, and the deed would have been done. Instead, they'd made sure things could go back the way they were as soon as I snapped out of the rut. They'd given me the option of pretending it never happened.

I closed my eyes. More bits and pieces of the recent past were filtering into my memory, blurred by the murky pall of madness. I'd been convinced Flynn and Jax were going to kill me. I would have killed *them*, given a chance.

My packmates.

My alefs.

I… I could have killed them.

My thoughts slid unpleasantly sideways, and the passage of time grew hazy. I opened my eyes, but I wasn't seeing the room. I was seeing a memory of Kameron Patel, his brown eyes sparking with frustration as he unleashed his pent-up anger at me.

You've already risked your lives! You've done it over and over—for us and for each other! There is literally nothing more you could sacrifice for us, simply because we were mated!

Jax or Flynn—or both—could easily be dead by my hand. I'd been a hairsbreadth from pulling the trigger on the Makarov and blowing a hole in Flynn's skull. If that had happened, how much comfort would I have taken from the fact that we didn't share a mate-bond through Leona?

A shudder wracked my body, and I wrapped my arms around myself as though I could hold all of my unraveling pieces together. The door opened, and I forced myself straight again. Flynn entered, bearing a plate with a sandwich and a bag of chips on it.

"Heya, alef," Flynn said. "Brought you some food." He set the plate down on the bedside table beside the water and the bottle of aspirin; then he flopped down in the chair Jax had vacated. "You know, you are one seriously terrifying bitch when you're rutting. Will you please mate the omegas now so we don't ever have to do that again?"

A choked sound wrenched free of my throat. In another life, it might have been the bastard offspring of a laugh. *God*, I was losing my fucking mind.

"Did you seriously strap one of your perverted sex toys into my mouth?" I asked in lieu of answering.

He shrugged. "Shit comes in handy sometimes—not that you ever really struck me as the leather-and-floggers type. Next time, leave the bondage gear for the guy who actually enjoys it."

I reached for the sandwich, mostly in self-defense. It was tuna salad—my favorite.

Flynn watched me with his dark eyes that always saw too much. I chewed and swallowed, aware of the heavy weight of the question I hadn't answered.

"I'll talk to them," I said. "Kam and Leona, I mean." The next words caught in my chest, and I had to clear my throat before I could get them out. "I don't want to lose this pack." It was a hoarse rasp.

Flynn blinked at me. "You're not going to lose this pack, alef. Who on earth made you think that?"

The stupid bitch in the mirror, I didn't say. Instead, I looked down and took another bite of my sandwich. "I'll talk to them," I repeated, mumbling the words around a mouthful of food.

As if my words had summoned them, Kam and Leona appeared in the open doorway. Flynn glanced over his shoulder at them before turning back to me.

"You do that," he said.

Leona came over and pressed a kiss to his short-cropped black hair. "Give us some privacy, Big Man," she said.

He caught her wrist and brushed his lips to it. "You bet, Sweet Thing. Get this mess figured out for us, okay?"

Flynn rose, grasping Kam by the nape of his neck and rubbing a possessive thumb over the bite scars at the juncture of his shoulder as he passed. The door closed, and I was alone with the omegas.

I set the sandwich aside.

Leona looked tired, but Kameron looked like absolute shit. And... he wasn't moving right. He was moving like someone in pain.

"They told me you weren't hurt," I said, horror and guilt snaking through me like cold water. How many times had I knotted him? Two? Three? "Kam, you look awful."

"Told you I should have come alone," Leona muttered.

Kam narrowed his eyes at me. "It's impolite to comment on an omega's appearance, *especially* after they help you through a rut. And by the way, you look like a two-day-old corpse yourself."

I opened my mouth. Closed it. Turned my gaze on Leona. "Is he hurt, though?"

"He's sore, because he insisted on letting you knot him three times in twenty-four hours," she said. "There's some minor tearing, but nothing that needed medical treatment. You should probably know that when it comes to you, he's a bit of an idiot."

Kam visibly ground his teeth. "I am standing *right bloody here*."

"Only because you're too sore to sit." Leona's tone was unapologetic.

"If it's any consolation, I think my clit is broken." I shouldn't be able to joke about this. Not with the dark circles of pain and exhaustion beneath Kam's eyes.

"I bet," he said.

I swallowed, my throat clicking. There was no point in putting this off. "You didn't let me bite you."

Silence settled over the room for a long moment.

"I thought about it," Kam admitted quietly.

"We're not saints," Leona said. "But we're also not monsters."

I could barely breathe. "I almost killed Flynn. I hurt you, Kam. If we'd been mated, none of this would have happened. You could have stopped me... calmed the rut."

"Yes," Leona agreed. "But fear and might-have-beens aren't a good enough reason to mate someone."

I stared at her like she might somehow have the answers I needed—my own personal oracle. "I'm losing my pack." It was a whisper.

She scowled, fierce as a hunting hawk. "*Never.*"

But Kam shook his head. "It's not that simple, Leo." He frowned at me, his sunken-eyed exhaustion doing nothing to blunt the edges of the expression. "You want to lose your pack? Then keep walking away from them like you've been doing for the last six months."

"Kam!" Leo sounded shocked.

"It's true," he said, refusing to break eye contact with me. "You don't want to mate us? Fine. But you'll have to come to terms with the fact that leading your pack now includes us as part of the deal. Of course, the real problem is that you *do* want to mate us. You have all along."

"*Of course I fucking do!*" The words erupted from me in a frustrated shout. I froze, but it was too late. They hung in the air, irretrievable and indelible.

"We want that, too, Alex," Leona said—the calm to my storm.

They wanted it, and they still hadn't stolen it from me when they'd had the chance. Because they were noble in a way I wasn't, and fearless in a way I desperately wished to be someday.

"I'll be horrible at it," I rasped. "You don't know what kind of a fucked-up bond you're signing up for."

"No offense, but you may be in for a bit of a shock when you get a peek inside Flynn's brain," Leona said. "The word 'twisted' comes to mind, along with a few others."

"And I, of course, am a paragon of mental health and solid coping skills," Kam added. "Though on the positive side, you'll probably only have to experience that part for a few days each quarter, around Leo's heat."

Wait. Had I just agreed to mate them? Had I really just done that? My entire body felt numb.

I licked my lips. "When is your next heat?"

"In six weeks," Leo said. "Well, five and a half now, I guess. So, is it a date?"

I tried to reply, but it took a couple of attempts to get words out. "I… yes."

I'd done it. I'd agreed to mate two omegas — to risk losing them in the future, as long as it also meant having them in the present. And… I'd done it in the crappiest possible way.

Swallowing audibly, I tried to do better. "I'm sorry, that sounds like I'm trying to put it off, but… Kam? Do you know for certain if Leona's heat pheromones were what caused the bond to form for you?"

He shrugged, pretending that the loss of the psychic bond after Leona's heat subsided hadn't broken his heart. "It's all guesswork at this point. But Jax bit me ages ago, and the bond flared to life as soon as he also bit Leo. I don't think I have to take the bite during her heat for it to work."

Leona's brows drew together. "But we don't know what happens if an alpha completes the connection through me when I'm not in heat. I mean — I know it would still work for me, but we don't know if it would make a difference for Kam."

I tried to sort through it with a brain that still felt as thick and useless as porridge. "Then we should wait. This isn't a high school science experiment. If making the connection while you're in heat is what definitely works, then that's what we should do."

This was surreal. Where was the pain? Where was the deep sense of existential dread?

Don't live in the past, Alex. You have a future waiting, too. You just have to reach out and take it.

That was what Irina had told me when I first discovered she was still alive. She'd tried to warn me not to cling to the trauma of our torn bond. I hadn't listened then, but maybe now I was finally ready to hear the truth behind the words.

"That's what we'll do," Leona said. "Kam?"

He nodded. "Agreed. Now, will you please move back here to the guesthouse, Alex? Because there's no more reason for you to stay away from us. Honestly, there never was."

Everything felt like it was crumbling around me—the collapse of a structurally unsound building finally succumbing to gravity. But... was there a possibility I could build something new on the rubble?

"Yes," I said. "If you really want me there, I'll come back."

SIXTEEN

Jax

TO SAY I WAS relieved was an understatement. Alex might still be a bundle of raw nerves, but she wasn't actively imploding anymore. Perhaps more importantly, she was *here*, where we could help.

Twenty-six days after the near-disaster of the conference in Belarus, I still couldn't quite get over the rightness of waking up in the morning as part of a messy, tangled pile of the people I cared about most in all the world.

I'd missed sparring with Alex, even though it usually meant getting my ass kicked. I'd missed the way Flynn's tightly held tension loosened a bit when he knew he could rely on our pack leader to make the hard tactical and ethical decisions. Mostly, I'd missed the security of trusting that our pack structure was stable; that we weren't going to shatter under the next unpredictable blow.

After the retrieval mission to get Beckett and the others out of Sloane's hands, I'd had a taste of what could be our future, and I'd wanted it—badly. Three alphas. Two omegas. A merged pack, with everyone playing to their

strengths and bolstering the others' weakness-
es.

We were so close—just a few more weeks.
And yeah, I was impatient... but I understood
and agreed with Alex's reasons for wanting to
wait until Leo's heat to finalize the mating.
Like her, I wasn't willing to play roulette with
Kam's limited ability to bond. This was how it
had successfully worked for him before, so this
was how we would do it again.

For now, though, there was the next conference to address. This one was going to be
bigger, and I wasn't sure whether that made it
more dangerous or less.

Nikolayev had been surprisingly successful in getting ahead of the story about the
drinks spiked with the drug targeting alphas.
He'd immediately put his pet doctor in front of
the cameras, citing the test results from Alex's
blood. They'd spun it as a dangerous psycho-
active chemical, and hadn't mentioned the
word 'rut' at all.

Other reports—originating from the BLF
or, just possibly, from Enoch Sloane's branch of
the Committee—had tried to float a narrative
about rabid, out-of-control alphas attacking
betas without provocation, but they were too
late. Nikolayev already had his version of the
story in place, backed up by science and foren-
sic evidence. That wasn't to say that the fringe
crazies weren't buying the BLF's account, but
your average person in the street understood

what had really happened—assuming they followed the news at all.

The prospect of a previously unknown terrorist organization operating across international borders to physically endanger high-ranking government officials—first in Romania and now in Belarus—had been enough to finally prod the West into action. Luca Fouchet, the guy Leo knew from Luxembourg, apparently had a fair amount of clout with his government. They'd agreed, on surprisingly short notice, to host a larger summit in Luxembourg City, where representatives and heads of state would discuss sweeping changes to alphomic policy. We were still waiting to find out if Prime Minister Fairbanks from the UFNA, or even someone from his Cabinet, would attend.

"They'll need to do a better job of screening the staff this time around." Alex still sounded understandably sour about it.

Alex, Flynn, and I were in the one of the guesthouse's spacious meeting rooms, discussing the security situation while Leo and Kam were off filming another of her press releases with Nikolayev. A knock came against the frame of the open door. I craned around to find Beckett standing there, with a tiny bundle cradled in the crook of his arm.

Flynn lit up like sunshine through the bond, and I didn't try to stop the smile taking over my face. Without a psychic connection, I couldn't be sure what might be going through Alex's mind. I hoped the presence of Beckett's tiny daughter didn't stir up bad associations with her own lost pups. If it did, she hid it well behind her usual cool facade.

"Heya, Boss," Flynn said. "So, the munchkin's finally ready to come out of the oven, huh?"

Anika Nikolayev had spent the first few weeks of her life in a portable neonatal incubator that her sire had ordered brought in as a precaution, when Beckett's pregnancy had begun suffering complications. To my knowledge, while she'd spent short stretches of time outside the incubator with her parents, this was the first time she'd been out of the sterile white room inside Nikolayev's private basement medical clinic.

"She's met her weight goal with an ounce and a half to spare, and her lung function is good," Beckett said, bouncing the tiny pup gently in his arm when she started to fuss. "I thought we'd make our first trip out of the house a short one and meet the rest of the family properly."

"And it also gives you a chance to pick our brains about the summit, because you're about to perish of boredom?" Alex suggested dryly.

"Yes, you got me. I'm slowly going insane in that damned room... so there's that, too," Beckett agreed, deadpan.

Flynn was already on his feet. "Fuck strategy meetings. I want to hold her," he said, approaching Beckett with his arms out.

I rose, too—drawn by the tiny bundle and the intoxicating smell of a new pup. "I'm pretty sure you're supposed to rein in the curse words around newborns," I told him.

"For what it's worth, she's a bit young to pick it up yet. When she does start cursing like a sailor, it will probably be in Russian." Beckett carefully handed his precious burden to Flynn, the pair of them taking care to support her head through the maneuver.

"There we go." Flynn cradled her against his massive chest, a low alpha purr rumbling up. Anika freed one pink arm from the swaddling, waving her fist around.

"Look at you, Little One," I murmured, tweaking the blanket aside an inch or two to reveal her scrunched-up little face.

Alex had also wandered over to look, though not to touch. "If you came for adult conversation, you probably should have left her at the house." Her tone was tart. "I don't think you're going to get much beyond cooing and baby talk from these two for a bit."

"Occupational hazard, apparently," Beckett said without rancor. "Speaking of which… *incoming.*"

I focused inward along the bond, where the sense of Leo felt closer than it had a few minutes ago. She and Kam appeared in the doorway, along with our Russian host.

Nikolayev's heavy brows drew together. "Solnishko. Should she be so far from the house?"

"Yes," Beckett said simply. "She should. And you're fussing again."

To his credit, Nikolayev didn't argue further. "So I am. Forgive me." He took a deep breath, visibly refocusing. "The filming went well. I believe our attempts at public messaging are still successfully outstripping our enemies'. Our last sweep of the major news media showed a promising uniformity regarding public condemnation of the terrorist action in Belarus."

He was talking to an audience consisting solely of himself, because Kam and Leo had already joined the rest of us in fawning over Anika. Flynn handed her to Kam, who settled her in his arms and gave her a soft smile that clenched something painfully in my chest.

If ever an omega had been meant to cradle newborn pups in his arms, it was Kameron Patel. I thought achingly of the nameless, faceless offspring I'd doubtless left behind in the breeding pens, and closed my eyes against the upswelling of rage at those who'd taken it on themselves to make human beings into commodities—like livestock to be bred or neutered as convenient.

"Aren't you just the most beautiful little girl who ever was?" Kam asked, as he and Leo bent their heads close together over the swaddled, wriggling infant.

I didn't need a terrorist drug to rouse every alpha instinct I possessed, urging me to take these two somewhere quiet and breed them until we had pups of our own running around the massive three-story guesthouse, filling it with shouts and squeals of youthful laughter. Never mind that it was irrational—Leo wasn't in heat right now, and Kam could never have pups of his own.

It didn't matter. Through the bond, I felt Flynn's thoughts running on parallel tracks to mine. Our eyes met with perfect understanding.

Kam stroked the backs of his fingers against Anika's soft cheek before handing her over to her sire. Nikolayev took her, his body language clearly communicating that no one else would be touching her for the foreseeable future, with the possible exception of his mate.

I wondered if she'd thrown up or peed on any of his suits yet.

"You were saying about the news media?" Alex said, raising an eyebrow.

"Yes, that part's been promising so far," Beckett replied, settling onto a comfortable chair by the fireplace. Like Anika, he'd had a rough time of things. He was still pale and his face appeared gaunt—but there was a sharp glint in his eye as he continued, "Personally, I'm more interested in the possibility of following the BLF trail. The Belarusian secret police succeeded in catching the operative who drugged the drinks. They took him into custody a couple of days ago."

"Did they now?" Alex said, the same light kindling in her green gaze, like a hunter spotting prey.

"I can at least still use a telephone, so I've reached out to some old contacts in Interpol," Beckett went on. "No real shock, but the guy isn't cooperating. Still, we know his identity from fingerprint records, and it makes me wonder what would happen if we started following the money trail."

"He was paid?" I asked.

"He was," Beckett said. "And not in cash, which would have been the smart thing to do. There are bank records. No doubt they'll be opaque as hell—shrouded in shell corporations and money laundering schemes. It's something, though."

"A lead is a lead," I agreed. "If we could somehow tie the terrorists directly to Sloane's operation—"

"That would be a very neat resolution," Nikolayev agreed. "But also extremely sloppy on his part."

"Plus, it's every bit as likely that the trail will lead back to someone in the Euro-Soviet branch rather than Sloane's branch," Beckett said. "If so, that would complicate matters more than it would simplify them. We need Kostya's wing of the organization to lead world governments toward a more liberal policy outlook."

"It's still better to know than not to know," I said.

Alex nodded. "I agree."

"I'll lay odds that Sloane's got a BLF connection," Leo said with conviction. "That doesn't necessarily mean he was in on the Minsk attack—but the fact remains that the Committee tipped off the Montreal police and let them know I was an unregistered omega. The only people who knew about me at the time were the BLF scientists who escaped in Romania. And—as much as I hate to say it—we may have chased Sloane further into the BLF's arms by hijacking the Euro-Soviet branch of the Committee."

"That's true enough," Kam agreed. "The BLF seems to be based in Eastern Europe. Sloane may see them as the only viable allies he has left on this side of the Atlantic."

"Succinctly put," said Nikolayev, with impressive gravity for someone soothing a fussing infant at the same time. "Our goal, for now, is to draw the Fairbanks administration into negotiations. Just as Sloane may be seeking new allies inside the Euro-Soviet Confederacy, we will need allies in the UFNA. Going forward, most of our messaging should be targeted toward that end."

"We'll tweak the talking points for the next few videos," Leo said. "For now, though, it's getting late."

"And it sounds like someone's hungry," Kam added, as Anika's fussy cries grew in both insistence and volume.

"She's always hungry," Beckett said wryly. "You're right, though. We'll leave you to your evening. Thanks for the adult conversation, even if it *was* interspersed with cooing and baby talk."

I smiled. "Anytime, Boss. We're just happy to see you up and about."

SEVENTEEN

Kameron

THINGS WERE GOING too well. I paced back and forth in the nest, hopelessly restless even though I wasn't the one going into heat. The dormant mate-bond was stirring into life at the back of my mind as Leo's pheromones thickened. Alex and the others would be here soon, ready to finally complete the circle of our pack of misfits.

Hell, Secretary Fouchet had even contacted us a few days ago to say that he was in talks regarding the summit with a member of Fairbanks' Cabinet. Seriously—things *never* went this smoothly.

"What if Alex changes her mind and backs out?" The words burst free without my volition. I kept pacing, not wanting to stop and look at Leo, radiant in her casual nudity as we awaited the alphas' arrival in the nest.

"At this point?" Leo said. "I imagine Jax and Flynn would cold-cock her again and carry her here."

"It's not a joke!" I paused and tried to focus on my breathing, knowing that it was only my fear making me lash out at her.

A hand grabbed the waistband of my jeans from behind and tugged. I toppled onto the semicircular couch with a grunt. The couch sat at the edge of the sunken nest pit piled with cushions and blankets, ready for use. Additionally, a king-sized four-poster bed with a canopy dominated the far end of the room. Maybe including a beta-style bed in an omega nest was a Russian thing, but I didn't like it. I hadn't liked it before, and I liked it even less now that I'd seen Alex tied to that bed, fighting her bonds for hours and hours until I worried her wrists and ankles would tear and bleed.

"Odama." Leo took my chin in her hand and physically turned my face to look at her. "Have you ever known Alex to say she was going to do something and then not follow through?"

I clamped my mouth shut, because of course the answer was no. I wasn't finished fretting yet, though. She sighed and kissed me. I could feel her growing arousal through the bond... and, more distantly, Jax and Flynn's. Closing my eyes, I let myself fall into it, experiencing my packmate's heat vicariously.

"Sorry," I murmured when she finally pulled away from the kiss.

She bopped my nose with hers. "I love you, odama. We all love you. And before long, we're going to remind Alex what it feels like to be loved—in body and in mind." Her fingers plucked at my shirt collar. "Don't you want to lose the clothes? The others are on their way."

I shook my head. "Flynn enjoys ripping them off me too much."

She snorted. "Whereas you don't enjoy it at all, of course."

"Did I say that?" Despite myself, my paranoia was beginning to fade. I could feel Jax and Flynn's emotions accurately enough to be able to tell that nothing was wrong. If Alex had done a runner, they'd be upset enough for me to feel it through the bond, I was sure.

Leo wrapped me up in a hug, throwing a leg across both of mine for good measure. I buried my face in her soft hair—focusing inward, because it was still such a novelty to feel the others inside my thoughts like this. Although it was difficult, I mostly resisted the temptation to think about the inevitable loss that would come when Leo's heat subsided and my body stopped piggybacking off of her elevated level of bonding hormones. I didn't want to tarnish what time I possessed with grief for something that hadn't happened yet.

A rough voice came from the doorway. "Jesus, I don't know if this is better or worse than walking in to find him eating you out." I looked up to find Flynn leaning an elbow against the doorframe, watching us.

"Is everything all right?" Alex pushed past him, entering the nest. She looked a bit pale in the face, but she was *here*.

"It is now," I said, with complete sincerity.

I felt Leo's smile of happiness before I saw it—a sensation like the sun coming out inside my mind.

"Come in," she said, formally inviting the alphas into the nest.

They did. Jax and Flynn wasted no time in stripping off their clothing and tossing it aside. Alex was dressed in a loose tank top and track pants. Her dark hair was down, and her nipples poked through the thin fabric, tenting it.

Leo's burgeoning lust washed through me. I closed my eyes to savor it, but only for a moment—there was too much to look at. She pressed a final kiss to the hinge of my jaw and untangled from our embrace, giving the others her full attention.

"I'm accelerating from zero to sixty toward heat-brain," she said, with mild, self-deprecating humor. "I blame you three for that. But while I can still think—Alex, I took my birth control injection last night. If you want to use condoms with me, that's fine, but the others won't be. I do draw the line at cervical caps, though. Those things are horrible."

Alex nodded, though something haunted flashed behind her expression. It was no surprise that she found the subject of birth control and pregnancy a difficult one, after the loss of her pups with Irina. We'd already talked about it in a general sense, however. She knew Leo wasn't courting pregnancy, but that she wouldn't be doing cartwheels in an attempt to prevent it, either. Or, at least, she wouldn't be doing cervical caps. Having been press-ganged into helping her remove and replace the damned things during her heat, I could confirm that they were a pain in the, uh, cervix.

"I understand," Alex said.

"I have a request," I said, before I could lose my nerve. "I want you to mate Leo first while I watch."

Alex settled knowing green eyes on me. "You want to make sure I won't back out of the bond. I can't really blame you."

I sighed. So much for trying to play it off as a kink. "Sorry, that sounded horrible, didn't it?"

She was spot on, of course. I couldn't bear the thought of having her bite me when it wouldn't mean anything real. If she bit me first, only to balk at biting Leo, I wouldn't have a true bond with her, only a scar. If she bit Leo first, though, I didn't think she'd hesitate to also bite me. For her, the hard part would already be over.

"No," Alex said. "I deserve that. Rest assured that I'll be mating both of you tonight, but you can watch me mark your odama first."

"Now hang on a minute," Flynn said. His mood through the connection we shared was light and teasing. "Who said you were monopolizing both of them tonight?"

Jax snorted. "You gonna throw down with her for first dibs, asshole? Good luck with that."

"Oh, come on—arm wrestling," Flynn said. "Best three out of five."

"No," Alex told him flatly.

Leo began giggling uncontrollably—proof positive that she was, in fact, starting to lose it as her hormones took over. She slid off the couch and crawled through the sea of pillows to Flynn, who watched with definite interest as she climbed up the length of his body, scaling him like a proverbial tree. When they were nose to nose, she fluttered her eyelashes at him, pouting. "You'll be busy. You have to keep Kam occupied while he's waiting for his turn."

He huffed a laugh, not buying her *innocent* act for a minute. "Guess you're right about that, Sweet Thing. He does seem to have an awful lot of clothes on right now, doesn't he?"

… And that was how I ended up kneeling on the floor, cushioned by a mountain of pillows—with my back braced against the footboard, my arms spread-eagled and my wrists loosely bound to the wooden rails. Flynn took great pleasure in ripping the front of my shirt open, sending buttons flying. He unfastened my fly with slightly more care, made a pleased sort of grunt when he confirmed that I'd gone commando, and pulled my half-hard cock free.

"Got something new for you, Ginger Tea," he said, producing a pair of small metal clamps connected by a chain. The toy had almost certainly come from the bottomless drawer of unspeakable items that he kept in the bedside table.

"Thought you'd sworn off nipple clamps," I managed, attempting valiantly to ignore the anticipatory gooseflesh that rose across my exposed chest.

"For me, yeah. Not for other people," he said, and clamped the first one into place on my left nipple.

I yelped. Then I yelped louder when the second one pinched my right nipple, igniting a phantom ache in the two nipples that were gone. Flynn grinned, pumped my half-hard cock a few times until it stiffened further, and let go, leaving me trapped and panting.

"There ya go. Enjoy the show for a bit." Flynn rose from his crouch and patted me on the head like a dog. "Jax and me will be over to fuck your mouth later if we get bored while we're waiting."

I knew, intellectually, how twisted it was that I got off on things like this. That didn't stop the low pulse of heat at the knowledge that they'd make good on that promise—using me to warm their cocks and otherwise ignoring me, as though I were a fuckable piece of furniture. The heat of excitement stemmed from the idea that I wasn't too broken for them to want to use. The alphas would take pleasure from my body, and it didn't matter in the slightest that I was sterile and scarred.

That knowledge had been enough to get me going even before the mating bond had been in place. Now, I felt like a starving man at a banquet. Other people's lust thrummed through my veins, and it would be like this for *days*. I couldn't physically keep up with it for the whole time, of course—not like Leo could. But she and Jax and Flynn had been learning my limits at the same time I had. They were becoming experts in stringing me along—stringing me out—to wring as much from my body as it could comfortably give.

Now, I hung like a debauched display from the bed frame—shirt and pants gaping, exposed to the others' view with my dick hanging out and my aching nipples clamped and chained. Jax and Flynn were too busy watching Alex and Leo to pay much attention to me now... but I was willing to bet they'd take turns fucking my mouth afterward until I was lightheaded from lack of air. Anticipation sent a new pulse of need through me, trying to further stiffen my omega cock.

In the sunken nest full of pillows, Alex peeled off her thin cotton tank top. I stared at the long, lean lines of her torso, thinking *she's going to be ours... we're finally going to be as we were meant to be. Pack.*

Her loose track pants followed. God—I wasn't ever going to get enough of seeing Leo and Alex together naked. Alex bent down, touching one fingertip lightly to Leo's jaw. She used the contact to draw Leo forward on her hands and knees toward the curved couch. When she reached it, Alex lowered herself onto the seat like a queen and drew up one leg, exposing herself to our gazes. I couldn't see Leo's expression with her back to me, but I could feel her giddy smile lighting me up from the inside.

"You like to mark your alphas?" Alex asked. "In that case, I want a line of love bites up the inside of each leg… right up to the top, little omega."

Leo pounced like an excited kitten with a ball of string, her joy and need shining through the bond like a beacon. Jax, Flynn, and I watched avidly as Leo bit and sucked her way up one hard-muscled leg, paused long enough to tease Alex's clit fully out of its sheath with her tongue, and then abandoned it to repeat the process on the other leg.

"Well done." The praise was practically a purr, and my mouth watered with the need to get my lips and teeth on Alex like Leo just had. *Anywhere*. I didn't care where.

Alex cupped Leo's chin again and directed her onto the couch, where she straddled Alex's lap. Leo cupped Alex's face between her hands, meeting her eyes from inches away.

"Are you doing all right, alef?" Leo asked solemnly, not yet too far gone for words.

Alex's expression made my chest ache.

"I'm terrified," she said. "But I also need my pack."

"You've already got us, Alex," Jax said. "You always did."

"This is going to be so much better, though," Flynn added. "You'll see."

Alex closed her eyes and bowed her head. Leo pressed their foreheads together. "Please fuck me, alpha. I need your knot… I'm so empty, and I want you to fill me up now."

Her perfume was filling the room in great clouds, proclaiming the truth of her need to every alpha in sniffing range. Flynn gave a low groan. Jax leaned back on his pile of pillows and wrapped a hand around his cock, shamelessly jacking off to the show.

Alex released a sharp breath and framed Leo's ribcage with long-fingered hands, bending her backward and leaning down until she could get her mouth on Leo's generous breasts. Leo gasped, her perfume growing sharp and musky as her body sprinted toward her first peak. With a playful, kittenish growl, she wriggled free, scooted up, and impaled herself on Alex's erect clit.

Alex let out a snarl that sounded considerably less playful. She twisted them both, depositing Leo on her back on the couch cushions. Hooking an elbow under Leo's right knee to draw her leg up, Alex set up a rhythm and pounded into her until Leo was gasping obscenities and clawing at her back in desperation.

"Oh, god… oh, *god*! Yes! Bite me, alpha! Knot me, *take me*!"

Alex pulled out, but only long enough to drag Leo down to the floor on her knees and reenter her from behind. I was drunk on Leo's rising peak and the alphas' lust—so much so that I almost missed it when Leo wailed out her first climax, and Alex sunk her teeth into Leo's neck, over her mating gland. The bright spark of pain knifed through the bond, too entwined with pleasure to be easily separated.

Everyone froze. Jax's hand stilled on his cock. The only sound was Leo's desperate panting and Alex's rumble of a growl, slowly modulating to a purr. A grin spread over Flynn's face.

"There you are, alef," he said softly.

"We missed you." Jax sounded deeply gratified.

A great, warm wave of relief washed over me. *The hard part was over.*

Hours later, with my lips swollen and my throat raspy from the others' use... with Alex riding me hard from behind and my capricious orgasm dancing just at the edge of my awareness, it was almost anticlimactic when Alex bit down over the silver marks left by three other sets of teeth.

Of course the five of us were always going to end up here. How could we not? It was meant to be. Pain flared as the skin broke, my blood mixing with her saliva. My body clenched, my mind whiting out with pleasure as I reached my release—and when my scattering thoughts reformed, there she was.

So damaged. So unsure. Her scars were every bit as bad as mine were—they were just hidden on the inside. I wished, as I always did, to be that last little bit closer to them in the psychic bond. But I was close enough. Love echoed through the shared connection, flowing back and forth, through and around — weaving us into a cohesive whole, no matter our individual broken parts and sharp edges.

Pack, at last.

EIGHTEEN

Flynn

THE PALAIS DE LA Cour de Justice in the Kirchberg quarter of Luxembourg City was one hell of a swanky venue. The building was the site of the Euro-Soviet judicial court, and evidently the Confederacy had thrown a fair amount of money at it.

The place was all polished wood, glass, and dark steel, with a weird fucking art installation in the center that looked like a floating yellow jellyfish and took up two entire stories in the main atrium. The summit was taking place in an audience hall that took up most of the second floor. It had the feel of a courtroom, but on a massive scale. A huge, raised area took up the front third of the space, and the rest was filled with long, pew-like benches for the onlookers.

The courtroom of the gods, I thought with a touch of sarcasm.

This was my first time in Luxembourg. Before prepping for this mission, the sum total of my knowledge about it was that it was tiny, and the language was some kind of bastard lovechild between German and French.

Well, that, and the fact that there was a politician here who secretly had the hots for Leona—but I wasn't allowed to corner him and put the fear of alphas in him because he was useful to us, or some shit like that. Didn't mean I wasn't keeping an eye on Secretary Luca Fouchet, though. One wrong move, and he'd learn the hard way that you didn't flirt with a mated omega. Just because he'd apparently been the one to talk Prime Minister Fairbanks from the UFNA into attending the summit wouldn't change that.

Aspects of this whole situation were kind of surreal. I mean, the whole point of going public with the fight against Sloane and his hard-liners in the Committee had been to get the struggle for alphomic rights onto the world stage. But it was still weird seeing alphas and omegas openly mingling with the beta elite, however cautiously.

There were officials here from parts of the world where the Committee held less power—an alpha prince regent from some tiny African nation I'd never heard of; an omega Māori MP from New Zealand; a mixed delegation of human rights advocates from Iceland. Additionally, there were dozens of alphas and omegas from different walks of life who'd been invited here to testify about the atrocities they'd suffered at the hands of the Committee's brutal laws.

Kam was one of those people. He was currently seated at a long table that had been set up on the massive stage in the audience hall, along with nineteen others who were scheduled to speak this afternoon.

Leo and Nikolayev were in the crowd of onlookers, which included delegations from over a hundred countries. Jax and Alex were watching Leo's back, and Beckett had Nikolayev covered.

I was on Kam duty with Irina, which was another bit of weirdness adding to the general sense of unreality surrounding the summit. If someone had told me a year ago that Irina Pasternak was not only still alive, but was also working for Kostya Nikolayev—and that I'd be sharing guard duty with her at an international conference—I'd have laughed in their face.

To be honest, I still wasn't one hundred percent over what she'd done to Alex. But ever since Alex had a heart-to-heart with Irina's beta mate, or husband, or whatever, she'd seemed to be doing better. The bond Alex, Jax, and I shared through Leona meant it was a lot harder for her to hide from us these days. And that was a good thing. She was still pretty messed up in the head, but who was I to say anything? We were all messed up in one way or another.

So, anyway, I could play nice with Irina for something like this summit. She was still one hell of a competent soldier, and it's not like she hadn't gone through a ton of trauma, too. If she'd found happiness—or at least peace— with a beta politician, then more power to her.

Her husband, Polonsky, seemed like a guy who mostly had his shit together. He was sitting with Leo and Nikolayev as the current speaker, a middle-aged beta woman, talked in a halting voice about the prison sentence she and her husband had served after failing to register their son when he'd presented as an alpha during puberty.

I wasn't thrilled with the distance separating us from Kam, in case anything went wrong. Private security hadn't been allowed on the stage, so we were down on the main level and off to one side. On a positive note, the staff for the event had been thoroughly vetted this time around. Even the attendees themselves had all gone through metal detectors and had their identities thoroughly checked.

"I didn't expect to see Beckett back on duty for this," Irina said quietly, as the beta woman on the stage wound down, receiving a round of sober applause from the great and the good in the audience.

I raised an eyebrow. "Did you think Nikolayev was going to lock him in the nursery or something?"

She snorted. "It had crossed my mind, yes."

"Nah," I said. "Beckett would have broken out, and then he would have been pissed. Besides, a bunch of Nikolayev's relatives descended on the place. They came to meet the newest addition to the family and got roped into babysitting. I think it's safe to say Anika is just about the safest pup on the planet right now."

Thinking of Anika always got me feeling broody. Well, *horny* and broody. It was still a bit of a sore subject with Alex in particular, but our pack was gradually moving toward the idea of pups. Ever since I'd seen Kam and Leo cooing over Beckett's munchkin, I couldn't get the picture out of my head. I wanted Leo pregnant. Like, *really* wanted it. And Leo hadn't said no.

"Lucky little girl," Irina said, and if she was thinking about her own lost pups, she didn't show it. "She's going to have that whole family wrapped around her little pinky finger."

"Ten bucks says she'll be ruling the world by the time she's thirty-five," I agreed. "She's gonna be terrifying in all the best ways."

I glanced over the crowd during the lull between speakers. Jax saw me looking and sent an *all's good* pulse along the bond. Alex was a watchful presence in the background, and Leo was focused intently on the stage. It was good having that connection with them. Reassuring. Just as it was frustrating as hell not to have it all the time with Kam, who still only completed the connection with the rest of us when Leo's heat hormones were in full swing.

I'd had a couple of thoughts about that, actually. Once things calmed down, I needed to have a word with Beckett, and maybe Nikolayev, too. As if things seemed like they were likely to calm down anytime soon. *Ha.*

Prime Minister Fairbanks was seated in the front row of the audience. His wife and fourteen-year-old daughter had traveled with him, though his younger boy had apparently stayed behind. Jennifer Fairbanks leaned over and put a hand on her husband's knee. They weren't that far away from us, and alpha hearing allowed me to make out her murmured apologies that she needed to take their daughter to the restroom. They left discreetly, a pair of bodyguards peeling away to follow them.

The beta official who'd been introducing each new speaker rose and walked to the podium. "Please return to order. Next, we will hear from Senajit Mandal of Kolkata. Monsielle Mandal is an omega with firsthand experience of the underground railway—a group dedicated to helping alphomic individuals escape from slavery to find new lives with forged documentation and new identities."

I frowned. Kam was also from Kolkata. None of the other people on the stage looked Indian, though. And then, Kam got up from his chair. He crossed to the podium and adjusted the microphone, clearing his throat and settling a sheaf of notes on the lectern.

"Good afternoon," he said. "I must begin by clarifying that my name is no longer Senajit Mandal. For all intents and purposes, Senajit died at the age of twelve, along with the rest of his family."

The crowd murmured.

Kam looked up, his soulful brown eyes playing over the assemblage of politicians and diplomats. "The Mandal family were alphomic purebreds. We traced our ancestry through dozens of generations, and had been influential in the Bengali silk trade since the sixteenth century. We relied on strategic alliances and a fair amount of bribery to maintain cordial relations with the beta-run government, as well as our neighbors in the region. That worked for a surprisingly long time… until the day it didn't."

Silence had settled over the echoing auditorium. Kam looked down, straightening his notes.

"When I was twelve years old, Committee sympathizers arrived at my home, dressed in black and armed with automatic weapons." He lifted his gaze again. His eyes were dry, but I was willing to bet I would have felt his grief through the bond if we'd been connected. "They rounded up all of the adults and took them into the courtyard, where they shot them. Armed men held my littermates and me at gunpoint inside the house, while they stripped us naked one by one to check our alignment.

He paused, swallowing. "My siblings were alphas. Vishaya, who used to love playing rugby. Jaina, who painted the most beautiful pictures with watercolors. Nalak, who was fascinated by our family's business, even at such a young age. At the time, they weren't deemed valuable enough to sell—there wasn't enough demand for alphas who hadn't been raised as slaves from birth. I was the only omega in the litter. I had economic worth as a breeder, so they chained me up, threw me in a cage, and dragged me off to the slave pens."

More murmuring.

Despite the fact that I'd been a slave on a breeding plantation myself before I'd been selected for the military alpha program, I *still* wanted to track down those vigilantes who'd put my Ginger Tea in chains and break every one of their necks.

"Breeding omegas on the plantations are chosen for genetics and temperament," Kam said. "My pedigree might have been impeccable, but evidently I fell short when it came to malleability. After one too many instances of insolence to my handlers, I was taken to a concrete room and strapped to a table. Doctors removed my womb and sewed me shut, ensuring that I would never be able to have normal sexual relations again. They cut out my extra nipples and attempted to remove my mating gland. When I didn't die from blood loss or infection afterward, they threw me onto the auction block, where I was sold at a discount as servant stock."

A few people rose and headed for the exits, looking ill. One woman began openly crying. I swallowed a surge of anger at the fuckers who were acting like this kind of shit was news to them. How oblivious did you have to be, not to know what happened on the production side of the thriving slave industry? Without omega breeders, there would be no docile, chemically castrated alphas to do the betas' unpleasant grunt work. Who the hell did they think was harvesting their vegetables, and processing their meat, and building their shiny buildings? Did they think alphas sprang into being from nothing, already fully formed?

Beside me, Irina was holding herself very, very still.

"Fortunately for me," Kam continued, "the woman who bought me was a member of the alphomic underground. She arranged for me to be sent overseas to the UFNA with a fake beta identity and enough money to start a new life. Senajit Mandal had already been dead for years. When I arrived in my new homeland, Kameron Patel was born. It would give me the greatest satisfaction to see a day when no other omegas ever need to suffer the way I did. I hope that this summit may—"

A hissing noise cut him off in mid-sentence, and for a split second, I thought it must be some problem with the sound system. Then heavy clouds of white vapor began to spew from the ventilation ducts in the walls and ceiling of the vast hall, billowing downward to cover the stage. I was already moving when the first screams reached my ears.

NINETEEN

Flynn

TWO FIGURES tumbled off the raised stage and fell to the floor, twitching. One was a big guy—probably an alpha. I didn't get a good look at the second before the clouds of gas billowed off the stage, obscuring the convulsing body. Then the beta woman who'd spoken before Kam staggered out of the obscuring vapor. She was limping but seemed otherwise unharmed as she ran toward the crowd in the auditorium, shrieking for help.

Irina's hand closed on my bicep, dragging at me until I turned to look at her.

"Stop!" she barked. "It's the VX agent. It has to be! Help the others get Alex and Leona out of here. If you go in there after Patel, you'll die. I'll get him."

Leo's terror and the others' shocked disbelief battered at me through the bond. "You'll die, too," I said stupidly.

"Maybe not," she said. Then she was gone—disappearing into the expanding fog.

I stared after her for the space of a heartbeat, my feet frozen in place. I knew I had to act. Jax would keep Leo from charging after

Kam, but Irina was right—if Alex realized that both Irina and Kam were in the gas, she might do something irrational. Jax would need help to get both of them out of here safely.

The gas was only feet away, creeping in white swirls toward my feet. Right on cue, Jax's wordless call for help echoed through the bond. I dragged my body free of its paralysis and sprinted toward the rest of my pack. Most other people in the audience hall were already running toward the exits, but Polonsky charged past me going the other direction… toward where Irina had disappeared into the gas.

For a split second I considered trying to stop him, but I didn't have time and he was a beta. If Irina was right about this being the BLF's experimental gas, he would probably be all right.

Leo was screaming. I thought it had only been inside my head, but no. It was in my ears, too.

"Let me go! Kam! *Kam*!"

Jax held her, and Nikolayev had a restraining hand around Alex's arm—which wasn't going to end well if he kept it there much longer. I charged in and knocked her off balance before she could break the Russian's kneecap and punch him out cold.

"Out!" I snarled. "Get the others out! Polonsky's a beta—he's gone after Kam and Irina!" I gave Alex a shove, knowing that if she fought back with any sort of force we were all going to be screwed.

Beckett appeared, white-faced. "This way," he ordered, in that tone we'd all learned over the years to obey without thought. *"Now."*

The gas rolled through the cavernous hall, spreading outward. Jax picked Leo up and bodily hauled her after Beckett, who had Nikolayev by the arm and was leading him in the wake of a tight phalanx of dark-suited security goons escorting Prime Minister Fairbanks toward the nearest exit.

I tamped down the mating bond as best I could in an attempt to try and keep my wits about me, but first I sent a silent prayer in Alex's direction—*please don't fight us.* With my hand clamped on her shoulder, I followed the others into the crush of people gathered in front of the double doors. It was exactly like fucking Belarus, except this time the bottleneck at the exit might end up being fatal for anyone stuck at the back, if the gas caught up with them.

A moment later, Beckett's strategy revealed itself. One of the UFNA bodyguards protecting Fairbanks roared, *"Move!"* When the knot of people in front of him didn't immediately clear, he lifted an arm and fired off a single gunshot at the distant ceiling. *"I said move!"*

The crowd around the door heaved forward in panic, erupting through the exit like a champagne cork being shot from a bottle. Beckett stuck to the back of Fairbanks' retinue like glue, and the rest of us followed suit. Bodies battered at me—other panicked attendees being tossed around by the tide of the crowd. I ignored them in favor of keeping a hand on Alex and an eye on Jax and Leona, while simultaneously slamming a heavy mental door closed on thoughts of Kam trapped in the cloud of experimental nerve gas.

If he was dead, there was nothing I could do except grieve him, and try to kill every bastard who'd ever given the Beta Liberation Front the time of day. If he wasn't dead, there was still nothing I could do. Not right now. I had to keep the others alive, and anyway, it would have been physically impossible to turn back and force my way through the press of humanity squeezing through the doors.

Leo's hysteria and Alex's desperate, toxic self-loathing throbbed through the bond despite my best efforts to block them, nearly drowning out Jax's cold determination to keep us safe. Beckett stayed right on the heels of Fairbanks' team, probably assuming that they would be heading for someplace secure.

Alex stumbled in my grip and heaved, upchucking whatever she'd eaten last. With Kam and Irina both possibly dead, I was aware that we were living her worst nightmare in vivid technicolor. Even so, I didn't release her or let her stop, half-dragging her along with me so we wouldn't lose sight of the others.

I hoped the UFNA goons were planning on getting their charge out of the damned building, because I couldn't stop picturing more clouds of gas erupting from the ventilation ducts above our heads. Fairbanks was shouting about his wife and daughter, demanding to know where they were. I tuned it out.

We eventually spilled out of a side door, and into a paved area beneath a large overhang. I silently congratulated the prime minister's goons on having chosen someplace that would hopefully stymie any terrorist snipers who might be waiting on nearby rooftops to pick off high-value targets as they attempted to escape the gas.

Alex jerked free of my hold and staggered backward against the glass wall of the building, sliding down it to the ground with a hand covering her face. Leo was sobbing in Jax's arms, still trying weakly to turn back the way we'd come as Jax held onto her from behind. Nikolayev's expression might have belonged to Satan himself, and Beckett was wearing a blank mask, his lips bloodless.

One of Fairbanks' bodyguards had two fingers pressed to his earpiece, listening. He looked up. "Sir, a car will be here for you in two minutes."

Fairbanks rounded on him. "I'm not leaving until someone tells me where Jennifer and Samantha are! Get me a damned report on my family—*now!*"

I remembered watching Jennifer Fairbanks excuse herself from the auditorium to take the kid to the restroom, right before Kam started speaking. They'd had security with them, and at least they'd been out of the room before the crowd panicked. Still, who knew if there were BLF operatives hiding elsewhere in the building who might've overpowered the bodyguards and snatched them.

"Prime Minister," Beckett said. His voice sounded hoarse, and he cleared his throat before continuing. "We have reason to believe that the attack used an experimental nerve gas designed to only affect alphas and omegas, not betas. There's every chance that they'll be unharmed, if they were even exposed in the first place."

Fairbanks didn't appear even slightly reassured—but he did pause, taking in Beckett's face for a beat before his gaze landed on Leona. Recognition dawned. "You..." he said. "You're..."

"Former employees of the UFNA government, yes," Beckett finished for him. "Until the Montreal Police Department raided Ambassador McCready's apartment at three in the morning, and threw her in a cell for the crime of having been born an omega."

The prime minister's bodyguards had been keeping a wary watch on us, and it grew even warier at Beckett's words. My packmates' raw emotions were still swirling around me. I did my best to stuff my own feelings in a box until we knew what was what. I felt the moment Leo's agonized fear and grief morphed into incandescent rage. She wrenched free of Jax's loose hold and raised a shaking hand to point directly at Fairbanks' face.

"*This!*" she shouted. "*This is the world you and your damned beta cronies have spawned. Are you fucking happy now?*"

TWENTY

Leona

THE MAN I'D believed in for so many years—the man I'd followed and worked for and *trusted*—gaped at me like a landed fish. Fairbanks' bodyguards closed around him, hands reaching into jackets where they were no doubt grasping their weapons, ready to draw.

Jax wrapped his arms around me again from behind and pulled me back a few steps. But I wasn't finished. I craned to meet Fairbanks' eyes past the wall of men in black suits.

"My closest friend may be *dead*! All because you and your fellow so-called leaders on the world stage couldn't commit to granting basic human rights to a tenth of the world's *fucking* population! You call *us* the threat?" I gestured furiously at the building we'd just escaped. "*That's* the fucking threat!"

Three sleek black cars pulled up to the portico where we were sheltering.

One of the bodyguards put a hand on the prime minister's shoulder and attempted to steer him toward the vehicle. "Sir, you need to get to a secure location."

Fairbanks threw the man's hand off. "I told you, I'm not going anywhere until I know my wife and daughter are safe!"

Beckett stepped between the two groups with a hand raised toward me in silent warning. "There should be a staging area set up somewhere in the complex to coordinate medical care for the injured, and hopefully act as a central hub for information surrounding the attack."

Nikolayev joined him cautiously, eying the twitchy security surrounding the prime minister. "We need to determine if the gas constituted the full extent of the attack, or if there are enemy operatives active in the area."

"Chairman Nikolayev," Fairbanks said, sounding calmer, but equally cautious. "Yes, that makes sense."

"Your transportation could be useful," Nikolayev continued. "Particularly if it's bulletproof transportation—just in case. It would be quicker and safer to drive until we find a checkpoint with radio communication to the venue's security center, rather than to trying to reach them on foot."

Fairbanks hesitated for only an instant, and then gave a single, decisive nod. "Right. Join me, please, Chairman. We'll track down someone who can get us answers." He turned his gaze on the bodyguards. "Keep trying to contact Jennifer's guards. Radio my driver the moment you learn something."

Beckett and Nikolayev exchanged a brief look that contained an entire conversation.

"There's not enough room for the rest of us," Beckett said aloud. "We'll hunker down here for now. Send a couple of cars for us as soon as you know where we need to go."

Nikolayev gave a sharp nod of acknowledgement and followed Fairbanks into the back seat of the middle vehicle. The bodyguards gave us a final mistrustful look and piled into the other two cars. Seconds later, the three black sedans drove off. Beckett let out an audible sigh and scrubbed a hand down the length of his face.

Just like that… there were no more distractions. The enormity of what had happened inside hit me anew, and all the strength left my legs. I would have crumpled to the concrete in a heap beneath the void of Kam's absence, if not for Jax's arms around me.

"Leona, see to Alex, please." Beckett's tone carried the weight of an order, woven through with empathy. "Jax, Flynn—with me. We need to keep a sharp eye out for any further trouble."

Jax supported me over to the glass wall where Alex sat slumped like a broken marionette and eased me down next to her. I was drowning, and so was she. It was all I could do to clutch at the solidity Jax and Flynn were offering us through the mating bond, knowing it was only their need to support us that was keeping them from going under as well.

"We're here for you," Jax murmured against my temple. He reached across and clasped his fingers around Alex's slumped shoulder. After a moment, he straightened and took up a watchful stance in front of us with Flynn and Beckett.

Alex stared into nothing, a terrible expression twisting her drawn features. I knew exactly what she was thinking. *Irina and Kam, both left behind.* If losing Kam was my personal nightmare, this was hers. We were both poised above a great, dark, empty space—suspended for the moment by uncertainty, but fully expecting to fall.

I turned into her, with no idea of how she was likely to react to the contact. The space she occupied in the pack bond was almost as much of a void as the space Kam should have occupied. And, *oh…* was that blank space where I wanted Kam more of a cruelty or a mercy? Outside of my heats, he was absent from our psychic link. If he'd been present like the others, we'd know if he was dead or alive—if he'd suffered and if so, how badly.

The thought was too much. My chest hitched with fresh sobs, my shoulders jerking as I buried my face against Alex's shoulder. Her left hand crossed her body to grab a fistful of my tailored suit jacket, and she turned her head until her cheek was pressed against my hair. A low, terrible noise wrenched free of her throat. Not tears; but rather, the sound of an animal in mortal pain. That sound reached into my very soul, finding its twin inside me.

I fisted handfuls of her clothing with the same awful desperation as she was holding onto mine, and we clung together while the others kept watch around us.

<hr>

Time felt meaningless, but the angle of the shadows beneath the portico had shifted noticeably by the time a pair of dark gray Mercedes pulled up to us and stopped. Dully, I recognized them as two of the official state vehicles Fouchet had provided us as a courtesy.

Beckett, Jax, and Flynn didn't immediately let their guard down. Alex barely reacted. The driver of the front car got out and exchanged words with Beckett before passing over a folded square of paper. Beckett unfolded it and scanned it quickly before giving a terse nod.

"There's a staging and triage area in the south concourse," he said. "Get in. We'll meet Nikolayev there. No news about our missing people yet—it sounds like things are still chaotic."

"No chance it's a trap?" Jax asked, eyeing the driver.

Beckett shook his head. "I recognize Kostya's appalling handwriting, and more importantly, there's a code phrase. Come on, let's move."

I wasn't sure if knowing Kam and Irina's fates would be better or worse than this all-encompassing uncertain dread, but there wasn't really much choice. We couldn't exactly stay here forever, huddling under an overhang. Jax took my hand and helped me stagger to my feet, swaying on rubbery legs like a newborn colt. To my surprise, it was Beckett who reached down and drew Alex up. Flynn was hanging back, both in my mind and physically. When I tried to catch his gaze, he looked away.

I ended up in the back seat of one car, with Alex in the middle and Beckett squeezed in on her other side. Jax and Flynn rode in the other car. The concourse was on the far side of the complex from the Palais de la Cour de Justice, but it was still only a couple of minutes' drive. We had to stop outside of the parking area, which was packed with ambulances, police cars, and fire trucks.

Covering the final distance on foot was complicated by the fact that I couldn't seem to feel my extremities. I was icy cold despite the perfectly pleasant late afternoon temperature, and it felt like there was a distinct lag time between ordering my muscles to move and getting a response from my body.

Beckett paused, his eyes playing over the chaos. He glanced back at us and jerked his chin, heading toward a large tent or awning that had been erected in one corner of the open area. I followed, clinging to Alex's arm, with

Jax and Flynn walking shoulder to shoulder a step behind us.

Nikolayev was waiting for us, standing at the edge of a knot of uniformed police and military officers. Several of them were in animated conversation with Prime Minister Fairbanks, who was still surrounded by his cadre of bodyguards as he railed at them. Nikolayev gestured us to an out-of-the-way corner, where we wouldn't be blocking the flow of official traffic in and out of the tent.

"News?" Beckett asked, in lieu of a greeting.

"There are casualties," Nikolayev replied grimly. "People trampled in the crowd, in addition to several presumed killed by the gas. No names have been released yet, although there has been a report that one of the Icelandic contingent is in critical condition with neurological damage."

His steel-gray gaze landed heavily on me, but I didn't feel the usual alpha pressure urging me to bend and show throat—I was too numb.

"All of the bodies are being taken to the morgue at the Hôpital Kirchberg," he continued carefully. "The most efficient approach might be to go there for identification."

He thought they were dead. *Of course* he thought they were dead. The gas had been specifically designed to kill alphas and omegas, and they'd been at ground zero of the release. But...

"The Icelandic representative is still alive." My voice sounded like rusty nails grinding together.

"And she is also being taken to that same hospital," he replied.

The sick dread ricocheting back and forth through the bond made it nearly impossible to think. Before I could come up with any reason why we shouldn't go to this hospital to look at a bunch of corpses who might be Kam, a disturbance cut through the increasingly angry exchange that was taking place between Fairbanks and the local officials.

"Levi!" It was a female voice.

I turned in a daze to see Jennifer and Samantha Fairbanks hurrying toward the UFNA prime minister, their ever-present bodyguards jogging to keep pace.

"Oh, my god." Fairbanks shoved past his own retinue to rush forward, catching his wife and daughter in his arms. "You're both all right?" He pulled back enough to cup his daughter's face in his hands. "Sammy? You're not hurt? You didn't get near the gas?"

"We didn't even know there *was* gas until a few minutes ago," Jennifer said. "Do you know what's happening? Who's behind this?"

"Sir, we need to get the three of you away from here," one of the security guards interrupted, and a moment later, the retinue headed out.

Irrational anger flared inside me, petty in its vindictiveness. How dare Fairbanks act so worried over his beta wife and child when we'd already told him the gas was designed to only kill alphas and omegas? How dare he get a happy ending while Kam and Irina were presumed dead? I could barely draw breath past the unfairness of it.

Nikolayev was looking after the reunited trio as well. "Pity," he said. "If Fairbanks had lost a family member in the attack, we might have successfully flipped the UFNA against Sloane."

Beckett eyed him. "Tell you what—I'm just going to pretend you didn't say that. Could we focus on the issue at hand, please? I want to make a sweep of the triage area before we leave for this hospital. It's big, but it's not *that* big."

"If you insist," Nikolayev said.

"It would put my mind at ease." Beckett gave Alex a concerned look. "I can go alone and report back."

"No," I said hoarsely.

"We'll all go." Jax sounded firm.

"I'll stay here to keep abreast of any new information regarding the attack," Nikolayev said. "Be as quick as you can."

I didn't actually want to do this, any more than I wanted to take a tour of a hospital morgue. But I trudged after Beckett nonetheless, aware of the others surrounding me. Alex was moving like a sleepwalker. Jax walked at her side with a supportive hand on her arm.

Flynn still looked lost inside himself, his presence muted through the bond.

Beckett led us along what I assumed was a logically laid out path through the confusion of the concourse, past knots of people standing around and rows of injured lying on makeshift pallets on the ground, waiting for medical attention. My eyes moved listlessly over the pale, shocked faces—hoping to see a familiar visage, but not really expecting to. Someone had called in a water truck. A line of people waited to be sprayed down with hoses—decontaminated as much as possible after exposure to the gas.

All of them were betas, I was willing to bet.

We'd covered slightly more than half of the crowded area when a gurney carrying a body bag cut a path toward the back of a parked ambulance nearby. My heart lodged in my throat as I watched the black bag juddering over brick pavers on its wheeled cart. I came to an abrupt halt—knowing that we should ask to see the body before it was hauled off to the morgue, but completely unable to move.

"I'll go," Beckett said softly. Before he could, Flynn sucked in a harsh breath.

I turned to look at him, following his gaze to a point some distance past the gurney with its tragic burden. All I could see for a moment was a man in a rumpled dress shirt with his back turned to us, standing near another ambulance. The others turned to look as well.

Beckett cursed sharply. "That's Polonsky. Come on—quickly."

Polonsky turned to look toward the ambulance. The movement revealed the shorter figure he'd been talking to, and my heart skipped a beat, my breath stuttering in my lungs.

Alex gasped.

"*Irina*," Jax breathed.

TWENTY-ONE

Leona

I WAS RUNNING before I even realized I'd moved. Flynn and Beckett were hard on my heels; Jax and Alex somewhere close behind.

Thank goodness I'd learned my lesson about wearing impractical stiletto heels to places that might be attacked by terrorists, or I probably would have broken an ankle. As it was, I slid to a halt, grabbing Irina by the arm with fingers that felt more like claws.

Polonsky looked alarmed in the instant before he recognized us, but then his shoulders sagged in relief. They were both soaking wet—they must have already been through the decontamination showers.

"Where's Kam?" I demanded, dreading the answer.

Irina took in my crazed appearance, her light-brown eyes dull with exhaustion.

"In the ambulance," she said, and I had a horrible vision of the body bag being transferred behind us. She jerked her head toward the vehicle parked a few yards away. "He was throwing up earlier, but they're giving him atropine to counteract the nerve agent. They think he'll be fine."

I blinked, trying and failing to take that on board. "H-how?" I managed. "How are—?" My voice cut off due to the blockage in my throat.

"How are we alive?" Irina's tone was sour. "It's just a theory, but the gas is designed to affect alphas and omegas. We're both neutered. There's very little left in us that's omega, from a physical or a hormonal standpoint."

"It was still a huge risk going after him," Beckett said quietly.

Irina shrugged a shoulder. "And what isn't, in this life?"

Polonsky had his fingers tangled with hers. "One day, you will do the wrong brave thing and end up dead, *Kachanaja*. And yet, I will still give thanks for whatever time we have together."

"You ran into the gas, too," Irina reminded him.

"Only because you are a terrible influence on me." Polonsky tore his gaze away from her. His eyes landed on Alex, and he frowned. "He is alive, my friends—I promise you. I'm so sorry we weren't able to find a way to contact you more quickly. I don't think the paramedics would appreciate five people cramming into the back of the ambulance, but I imagine they will allow one person to ride along to the hospital."

I'd been paralyzed in place like a statue, terrified that if I made a move toward the ambulance, I'd jerk awake to find that this was all a dream, and Kam was dead. Alex squeezed my hand. I hadn't even realized she'd been holding it.

"You should go." Her words were raspy, but I could feel her mental presence unfolding from its defensive huddle within the bond. There would be psychological fallout from this horrific near miss—not just for Alex, but for all of us.

Now, though, I needed to see my odama and make certain this was, in fact, real. I nodded. "Meet us at the hospital."

"We'll be there," Beckett promised.

I met Jax's blue eyes, and then Flynn's brown ones. Jax's gaze held the relief I expected, but Flynn's expression was still closed off.

"Go," Jax said. "We'll be right behind you."

I nodded, turning and walking toward the back of the ambulance like a zombie. Unsure of the proper protocol, I knocked on the closed metal door. It clanked open a moment later, and a harried woman in scrubs leaned out. She said something in a language that wasn't close enough to German for me to make out the meaning, the sentence rising into a question. Luxembourgish, probably.

"I need to see your patient," I said in French. "Please—I'm a family member."

"Leo? Is that you?" The weak voice came from inside the ambulance, and my heart clenched. I swallowed hard, forcing down a sob.

The paramedic looked over her shoulder, and then back at me. She gave a brisk nod. "Get in," she said, this time in French. "You can sit with him during the journey."

I scrambled into the back without an ounce of grace, where I found Kam lying on a gurney with an IV in one arm and a blood pressure cuff strapped around the other. He was pasty gray beneath his olive complexion, but his eyes were wide open and aware.

"Kam," I croaked, aware that if I broke down and started sobbing into his chest, I'd probably get kicked off the ambulance in short order.

"*Odama*," he said. "Is everyone all right? I'm so sorry I scared you."

I bit my lip hard and nodded, taking the bench seat the paramedic indicated and squeezing Kam's forearm. "They're okay. Just really worried. Irina's okay, too."

"Good." He sighed heavily. "I won't lie. When I saw the gas, I thought it was curtains."

My fingers clenched convulsively. "Irina said it didn't affect you as badly because of what was done to you both."

"Apparently so," he agreed. "She and Polonsky dragged me out of the auditorium. Maybe I took a bigger hit because I still have my mating gland and she doesn't."

It made sense. I also couldn't have cared less about the details right now. "As long as you're going to be okay," I managed.

"So they tell me," he said, as the ambulance rumbled to life and rolled forward. "It's too bad we were so far from help when Jax got dosed in Romania. If he'd gotten atropine sooner, maybe he wouldn't have had such a tough recovery." He let his head roll back, staring at the ambulance ceiling. "God. What is this going to do to the talks?"

"I don't know," I said. I almost added that I didn't care, either—but that wasn't true. I did care, and we'd be dealing with that part of things soon enough. "There are going to be a lot of angry world leaders. Fairbanks' wife and kid were missing in the confusion for more than an hour before they got reunited."

Kam winced. "Ouch. Someone's ass is getting fired over that, I'll wager."

"Probably," I agreed. Something about that reunion was still niggling at me, but it could wait. "The question will be whether all that anger gets directed at the terrorists, or somehow comes back on us."

He closed his eyes, sliding his arm up until I was holding his hand, our fingers intertwining. "That's a question for tomorrow, not today. I expect the doctors will want to keep me in the hospital overnight, at the very least. Are the others following us?"

"They'll meet us there."

He squeezed my hand, and I was relieved that his fingers didn't seem to be shaking or twitching. "Good."

Silence settled, broken only by the paramedic bustling around, taking readings and adjusting the IV drip.

"Is Alex okay, really?" Kam asked into the lull.

I chafed my thumb over his knuckles. "I mean… no, not really. She thought we'd lost both you and Irina. But Irina's okay, and once she sees you for herself, it will help even more. Flynn's struggling, too. Jax was upset before, but now he just feels relieved."

Another deep sigh. "God, I wish this hadn't happened."

"Me, too," I said, and hesitated before continuing. "I, uh, might have cursed out our old boss directly to his face," I admitted. "At extremely loud volume."

Kam opened bloodshot eyes to look at me. "You yelled at Levi Fairbanks?"

"I was upset," I said, by way of defense. "And I'm not sure any of it really penetrated, since he was busy freaking out about Jennifer and Samantha being missing at the time."

Kam mulled that over for a moment. "Well, it's not like he can fire you."

"True."

The ambulance rolled on, toward the hospital with its grim collection of gassed bodies stacking up in the morgue.

Kam had been right that the doctors would hold him overnight for observation. I had no idea what strings Beckett and Nikolayev had pulled—or what threats they'd delivered—but he ended up in a private room despite the heavy onslaught of patients in the wake of the attack. More importantly, no one came to kick the rest of us out when visiting hours ended.

There was a television inside the room, but I'd declared a moratorium on any news reports until morning. If something needed doing on that front tonight, it would have to fall to Nikolayev. Beckett had headed out after ensuring that we were settled for the night, leaving the five of us alone except for the regular check-ins from the nursing staff.

Kam had been taken off the IV drip, but was still hooked up to several monitors. A harried doctor had come in at one point to look at Kam's chart, scribble something on it, and inform us that if he continued to improve, he'd be released the following day.

The room only had two chairs for the four of us, but given how overwhelmed the hospital staff must be, no one wanted to make a fuss about it. There were extra blankets, at least, so Jax and Flynn had camped out on the floor.

Alex's mental presence in the bond evened out somewhat as the hours passed, but she was still mostly monosyllabic. She held Kam's hand in hers like it was made of glass, and none of us had tried to push her into talking. I desperately needed a good cry, but somehow this didn't feel like the time for it. The surroundings were too impersonal, and the others were too far away, sitting on the uncomfortable floor.

Flynn was worrying me the most right now. In fact, he was worrying me badly enough that I wasn't willing to let it slide any longer.

"Flynn, will you talk to us, please?" I asked, sending a nudge of concern along the bond. "We're all okay now—or we will be soon, at least. It's worrying me that you don't seem more relieved about that."

"I'm relieved," he said. "Not sure I've been this relieved since we got you back from the Montreal police, Sweet Thing. You don't need to worry about me."

I tried to find a new angle of attack, not buying it for a second. But before I could, Alex spoke up.

"He's beating himself up for not having charged into the gas cloud after Kam and Irina," she said.

My gaze jerked back to Flynn, appalled at the idea that he'd blame himself for that. It would have been suicide.

"Is that true?" Kam asked.

Flynn, who was propped against the wall near the door, shrugged one broad shoulder. "You know how it is. We're supposed to go after the ones who are in trouble. That's the deal."

"If you'd tried to come after me, you'd be downstairs in the morgue right now," Kam said. "I'd still be alive, and then I'd have to live with the knowledge that you threw your life away for me."

Flynn met his eyes, his expression narrowing. "Think I wouldn't die for you, Ginger Tea? Or for anyone else in this room? I would, you know. Hell, I'd do it with a smile on my face."

And what on earth were you supposed to say to something like that?

Alex shifted uncomfortably in her chair. "If you hadn't helped the others drag me out of the auditorium, I might have charged into that gas after them."

"I know," Flynn said. "That's what Irina told me to get me to turn around."

Jax, seated next to Flynn on the floor, drew in a deep breath. "I think... in many ways it's hardwired into us, as alphas, that dying is somehow noble, even if it's a pointless death. I've been in that place before—thinking that there was nothing I could do to protect the omegas in my care, so I might as well do something stupid and violent that would result in me getting killed. As though, by acting recklessly, I could at least ensure that no one would look back and wonder why I didn't do more."

With a pang, I remembered a terrorist cell... an impossible situation. "I told you in

Romania that you wouldn't help any of us by getting yourself killed."

"You did," Jax agreed. "And even if I knew it was true, objectively… I still didn't really believe it."

"I wouldn't want your death on my conscience, Flynn," Kam said. "Not ever. But even if I'd died in that gas, I would have wanted you to stay alive so you could help comfort the others while all of you grieved me. Not to die trying to save me."

"I'm supposed to protect you," Flynn said miserably.

"Sure, when you can," Kam agreed. "But sometimes you can't. If you can't, then like I said—I'd want you alive to be with the others, because you're more than just a glorified bodyguard. You're our mate."

Flynn's face twisted. He covered it before I could see the tears, but I knew they were there. Something in the tenor of his thoughts made me think he wouldn't be able to handle it if we all went to comfort him right now. I wanted to go to him anyway, but Alex gave me a small shake of the head. Instead, I watched as Jax scooted closer and slung an arm across his bowed shoulders.

"For what it's worth, asshole… I promise not to give you a hard time if you ever get killed doing stupid alpha shit," he said. "I get it."

"Fuck off," Flynn told him—but he didn't move out from beneath Jax's companionable, one-armed embrace.

The room fell quiet, but it was a comfortable sort of quiet. Exhausted, I leaned forward and laid my head on crossed arms at the edge of Kam's bed, trying not to worry about what tomorrow would bring.

TWENTY-TWO

Leona

THE FOLLOWING DAY brought Kam's release from the hospital, along with the news reports I'd insisted we avoid overnight.

SUSPECTED TERRORIST ATTACK KILLS 23 – DOZENS INJURED.

CHEMICAL WEAPON ATTACK DISRUPTS SUMMIT ON ALPHOMIC RIGHTS.

VIOLENCE HITS ALPHOMIC CONFERENCE – AGAIN. DISTURBING PATTERN EMERGES.

On the hotel room television, a BBC chat show nattered in the background as a man and a woman, both with smart suits and cut-glass vowels, lobbed speculation back and forth.

"At some point, Nigel, we have to start asking why these people are so intent on convincing us they're not a threat, when this kind of violence seems to surround them constantly."

"Now, Josie – that hardly seems fair when most of the victims in this attack were alphas and omegas. Yes, it's true that several betas also died during the panic inside the auditorium, but analysts are saying those deaths were in the nature of collateral damage – they weren't the real targets."

"And how much 'collateral damage' are we as betas going to be expected to take, while this endless debate rages on and on, Nigel? I don't see how we can be expected to..."

I tuned out the infuriating circular argument. Except for Kam, none of us had gotten much in the way of sleep over the course of the last day. Nikolayev and his network of Eastern European cronies were taking point when it came to the media, but sooner or later I'd be expected to release some kind of statement. The amount of makeup required to make me presentable for the camera was going to monumental, as was the self-control I'd need in order to produce anything more nuanced than the same stream of profanity-laced vitriol I'd unleashed on Levi Fairbanks.

At the time, he'd brushed me off with the practiced air of someone who got yelled at a lot in public venues. The thing was, I still felt like something had been off with him yesterday. It had been percolating away in the back of my mind as I dozed at Kam's bedside in the hospital, and also today, as we readied for a meeting with Beckett in what I desperately hoped was a secure hotel room.

When he arrived, it was with the air of a hunting dog on the scent of prey.

"There's news," he said without preamble. "It's significant."

"Let me guess." I couldn't keep the sour note from my voice. "The summit has been put on hold indefinitely due to ongoing security concerns."

"Rather the opposite," Beckett replied. "Fairbanks has been lobbying the other leaders not to leave Luxembourg yet. He's also requested a private meeting with you and Kostya."

I stared at him for a long moment. "Excuse me?"

"You heard right. Tonight at seven p.m., his hotel, no press." Beckett raised an eyebrow. "I would strongly suggest agreeing."

"Well," Kam said. "That's certainly... unexpected."

"Maybe you finally got his attention," Jax said wryly.

"By screaming obscenities at him?" I asked. "If I'd known that would work, I could have done it a year ago."

"Did he specify the reason for the meeting?" Kam said.

"No, although it's a fair guess it has to do with the attack," Beckett replied. "I don't get the impression that the major powers have been taking the BLF seriously until now."

"Well, that's something, I suppose." I tapped a finger against my chin, already plotting ways to maximize the potential benefits of this unexpected good news. "What's Nikolayev's take on this?"

"It's a foot in the door," Beckett said. "Kostya always plays his cards close to his chest until he sees how the other parties are approaching the situation. But the goal remains the same as it has been—drive a wedge between the UFNA and Enoch Sloane; get actual legislation on the table in the UFNA legislature, as well as in Western Europe."

"Right." As Beckett had said, in many ways the attack yesterday had changed nothing. But in others, it might have changed everything if Fairbanks now saw the BLF as an existential threat to be dealt with. "Count me in—as if there were any question. When do I need to be ready to leave?"

Kam frowned. "You mean, when do *we* need to be ready to leave."

"Oh, *hell*, no," I said. "Kam—they let you out of the hospital because they're packed to the gills with casualties, and you're a second-class citizen who isn't on the verge of death. But you were treated for nerve agent exposure less than twenty-four hours ago, and you're not setting foot out of this hotel room until you have *fully recovered*."

He drew breath to argue.

I cut him off. "Also, I intend to use you like a cheap whore when it comes to playing the sympathy card with Fairbanks. '*Oh, Prime Minister—I'm sure you remember Kameron Patel's speech—he was speaking right before the attack. Yes, he's still recovering… it was terrible! We were sure that we'd lost him,*' and so on."

"Damn, I love it when you're a manipulative bitch, Leo," Flynn said. "I am *so* hard right now."

"Too much information, Flynn," Beckett offered. "You're right, though. It could be a useful angle."

"We're going with you, of course," Alex said. "As security."

"If I'm stuck playing invalid, I want Flynn here with me," Kam said firmly. "I'll need security, too, after all."

I met his gaze and raised an approving eyebrow. *Now* who was being manipulative?

"Good idea," I agreed, knowing that the pair needed some time alone. Maybe then, Flynn could reassure himself that Kam really didn't blame him for not running into the gas cloud after him.

This was confirmed when Flynn's brow furrowed in a worried frown. "You sure you want me and not one of the others?"

"If I wanted one of the others, I wouldn't have asked for you," Kam said, with some asperity. "Look at it this way—I know you're still feeling guilty, which means I can make you wait on me hand and foot and you won't complain about it."

Flynn's face cleared. "Oh. Yeah, okay. I can do that."

"If that's settled," I said dryly, "then it looks like I've got a few hours to get some food, get my head on straight, and plaster on enough concealer to make it less obvious that I slept in a plastic hospital chair last night."

Beckett nodded. "We'll be back at six p.m. sharp with a car. Remember to place your room service order through the concierge. He's been thoroughly vetted."

With that, he left. Beckett had been taking every precaution with our security after the drink-spiking incident in Belarus. Our track record with staying one step ahead of the BLF was less than stellar at this point, but I still trusted whatever plans Beckett had personally overseen. We'd had a handful of meals here since arriving in Luxembourg City three days ago, and we hadn't been drugged or poisoned so far.

At this point, that counted as a win in my book.

"Who's hungry?" I asked, girding myself to tackle a private meeting with the man I'd publicly upbraided at full-scale 'shrieking harpy' volume only yesterday.

———◆———

Nikolayev was waiting for me in the back seat of one of the two cars that arrived to pick us up. His expression was a cool mask, giving nothing away. His charcoal suit was impeccable, and his Mephistophelean salt-and-pepper beard had been trimmed to razor-sharp lines.

He looked every inch the terrifying Committee kingpin I'd once believed him to be, and very little like the doting alpha sire who'd bounced a tiny girl-pup in his arms at two in the morning to soothe her colic.

Meanwhile, I probably still looked like an overstressed fugitive omega who'd spent part of the previous day believing one of my soulmates to be dead, followed by a restless night in an overcrowded hospital room wondering if my life's work had just circled the toilet drain and disappeared into the sewer line of history.

But I'd also had a revelation. It had hit me in the middle of my shower, where most of the best ideas come from. I considered telling Nikolayev and decided against it. If I whipped this one out later, I wanted it to pack the greatest possible punch. Conversely, if I was one hundred and eighty degrees off base, it would be better if I was the only one who looked like an idiot, rather than both of us.

We arrived at the prime minister's hotel at six thirty-five. The security checks involved in getting to him were as thorough and involved as one might expect. The five of us were escorted into a small conference room with guards stationed both inside and outside the door. I was confident that the space had been thoroughly checked for bugs as well as any potential threats—including, no doubt, anything hidden in the ventilation ducts.

Fairbanks rose politely as we entered. His day had been somewhat less harrowing than mine had been yesterday, since his family hadn't ended up in a hospital. Still, his practiced public face appeared a bit worn at the edges, and I was pretty sure I wasn't the only one in the room wearing concealer.

"Chairman Nikolayev," he greeted. "Ms. McCready."

"Prime Minister," I replied. "Thank you for inviting us here today."

Some people might have said I should lead with an apology for my outburst the previous day. I had no intention of doing so, for two reasons. First, I'd meant every goddamned word I'd said. And second, if he'd been as offended as all that, one might assume he wouldn't have invited me to this meeting.

Bowing and scraping had never gotten alphas and omegas anywhere. Unless we approached the table as equals, our ambitions of meaningful reform were doomed.

"Prime Minister," Nikolayev greeted—taking the seat Fairbanks indicated, as I did the same. "Your request to speak with us privately was, shall we say, somewhat unexpected. What is it you wish to discuss?"

Alex and Jax took up watchful positions along the back wall. Fairbanks reseated himself across the conference table from us, steepling his fingers before him. "May I be frank, Chairman?"

Nikolayev slanted an eyebrow. "I hope you will be."

Fairbanks gave a single nod, as though to himself. "In that case, I wish to discuss Enoch Sloane."

"A disagreeable subject, but a necessary one," Nikolayev said. "May I assume he contacted your administration before the summit began?"

"He did." Fairbanks tapped his forefingers together, and let his hands fall to rest on the table. "He threatened to topple the current parliamentary coalition if the UFNA agreed to any major pro-alphomic concessions during the talks."

"The Committee threatens the same thing *anytime* there are talks regarding the current laws," I pointed out. "They've done that for years."

"Yes." Fairbanks frowned at us. "But this time, he also had some very specific allegations aimed at you, Chairman. I wanted to speak with you directly for that reason." He squared his shoulders, as though steeling himself. "Are you an alpha, Chairman Nikolayev?"

Nikolayev didn't so much as blink. "If I were, how would that change the course of our discussion?"

Fairbanks drew breath, only to hesitate. "There are reports," he said slowly, "of actions you've taken in the past that seem... at odds with your recent policy changes within the Euro-Soviet branch of the Committee."

That was as diplomatic a way of asking why someone would brutally murder a family member for being an omega, and later crusade for increased alphomic rights, as I was ever likely to hear.

"Reports may sometimes be misleading." Nikolayev's tone was mild. "One wonders what sort of world would voluntarily hand over power to such a murderous individual."

"A troubled one," Fairbanks replied.

The same haunted look I'd noticed yesterday was back in his eyes—and this was the moment. It was time to drag out the heavy artillery and find out if it would explode in my face or not.

"You have a very good reason for wanting to know if the stories about the Chairman are true," I said. "Don't you, Prime Minister?"

Fairbanks' jaw tightened, his closed expression growing rigid.

"For you, it's personal," I continued. "You know, you really are an exceptional actor. I was in your administration for *years*, and I never even suspected."

Now Nikolayev was staring at me as well, his sharp brows drawn together.

I met Fairbanks' eyes and delivered the *coup de grace*. "This hits directly at your family, doesn't it? I saw the way you reacted yesterday, when you thought they might have been exposed to the gas. Your daughter, Samantha, is an unregistered omega."

TWENTY-THREE

Kameron

THE INSTINCT TO soothe upset alphas was hardwired into omegas from the time we were pups. Some betas—and some omegas, for that matter—found the idea demeaning. Maybe it was my purebred upbringing, but I never had. Yes, the urge could rear its head at inappropriate times. So could every other ingrained biological urge one might care to name. That was simply *life*, busily doing its thing at the cellular level while we weren't paying attention.

Personally, I found a certain beauty in the way alphas and omegas meshed. Flynn's reaction to not having thrown his life away in a doomed attempt to drag me to safety was basic *Alpha 101*. Honestly, I'd been surprised by the depth of self-awareness our three alpha mates had shown when discussing it. They understood—intellectually, at least—that getting themselves killed pointlessly and unnecessarily wasn't helpful to anyone. However, understanding something intellectually wasn't an instant cure for feeling like shit about it.

That was where omega soothing came in, and it wasn't as though it was a hardship in this particular case.

I did, in fact, still feel like hell. If Leo hadn't put her foot down, I was sure I could have successfully ridden in a car to the prime minister's hotel and sat at a table for an hour or two. However, it wouldn't have been nearly as enjoyable as lounging on the hotel bed with Flynn, bracketed by his tree-trunk thighs with my back resting against his broad chest while he fed me petit fours by hand.

"Ugh, *mercy*," I said. "Seriously, stop. I'm stuffed."

He set the tray on the bedside table without so much as jostling me, then started stroking my hair away from my temples like someone stroking an exceptionally well-fed cat.

"You don't feel sick again, do you?" he asked.

"Not nauseated or anything like that, no," I assured him. "Just tired, and like my body weighs a ton."

"You didn't eat *that* much," Flynn said.

I snorted. "I think it has more to do with the damned gas than the food. Give me a few days and I'll be right as rain." I shifted with a sigh, pressing my head further into the contact of his rhythmic petting. "Frankly, I'm more worried about the fact that I didn't get a decent sex joke out of you in response the 'stuffed' remark. That opening was as wide open as my asshole after Jax finished knotting me."

His chest shook with silent, surprised laughter. "Didn't really seem like the time, Ginger Tea," he said, his arms coming around me from behind in a hug.

I relaxed into it, thinking for the hundredth time that I'd never expected to have this much out of life. The past few months had been harrowing, but they'd also brought blessings beyond my wildest imaginings.

"Can we talk about something?" Flynn asked, surprising me.

"Anything," I told him. "Always. What do you want to talk about?"

"You," Flynn said. "I was gonna have a word with Beckett first, or maybe the Russian. But now I think that was wrong and I should ask you first."

That sounded a bit alarming, but I only said, "What about me?"

His barrel chest rose and fell behind me, lifting my torso like a ship riding a wave.

"So… they make drugs and stuff for omegas, right? Heat blockers and pheromone suppressors and the like."

"Yes?" I replied cautiously.

"I was just thinking—what if you could get, like, hormone replacement therapy, only for omegas?" he said. "Would you want that?"

I blinked. My mouth opened, but nothing came out. After a moment, I closed it.

"Hormone replacement therapy?" I echoed eventually.

"Well, you take testosterone now, don't you?" Flynn said. "To keep that pretty beta physique. What if, instead, you took the hormones that your body would have been producing, if the beta butchers hadn't caught you as a kid?"

"I… don't know," I replied blankly.

"Like, what if you could take omega hormones, and it meant you were able to stay in the bond all the time instead of just when Leo's in heat? That's what I was thinking."

Again, I paused… struck dumb.

"I don't know," I said again, trying to push past my surprise. "I'm not aware that omega hormones are even available on the black market."

Flynn breathed out. "That's why I wanted to talk to Beckett and Nikolayev. They've got a direct line to the good stuff, so I figured they'd know if it can be done or not."

I lay in the alpha's arms, not sure if it would be too painful to contemplate the what-ifs, in case it wasn't possible to procure omega hormones or they wouldn't work for someone like me.

"Give me some time to think about it," I told him, after long moments had passed in silence.

"'Kay," Flynn said easily. He slipped a hand down to tug at the elastic of my waistband. "Now get these stupid pajamas off. You're all tense. I wanna give you a massage."

"Oh, very well. If I must." My long-suffering air sounded fake enough to draw a snort of amusement from him.

He nudged me forward so that he could slip out from behind me and retrieve a small bottle of massage oil from his luggage. I managed to overcome my heavy limbs long enough to strip off the flannel pajama bottoms and white T-shirt I was wearing by the time he returned.

A massage from Flynn was never going to be PG-rated, but even when his oiled hands wandered to places that made me squirm and gasp, there was no indication that I was expected to do more than relax and enjoy it for what it was—alpha caretaking at its finest.

Within half an hour, I was a puddle in the center of the mattress. Evidently, having absolutely no muscle tone anywhere in my body was somehow conducive to making emotionally fraught decisions.

"Flynn?"

The alpha's big hands stilled on my back. "Yes, Ginger Tea?"

"Talk to Beckett and Nikolayev," I said. "I want to know if it's possible."

TWENTY-FOUR

Leona

"YOUR DAUGHTER Samantha is an unregistered omega." The words landed like bricks in the dead silence of the conference room. I heard Jax and Alex's sharply indrawn breath at the same instant their shock hit me through the bond, and Beckett said, "*Ah,*" in a quiet voice of revelation. Nikolayev's sharp eyes swung to Fairbanks to gauge his reaction.

That reaction was both startling and completely unmistakable. The UFNA prime minister shoved to his feet so abruptly that his chair toppled backward. His hands gripped the edge of the table so tightly that the knuckles turned white.

I saw the moment he realized what a giveaway his response had been. His gaze flew to the blank-faced security guards posted around the room. A couple of them had stepped forward in alarm upon seeing their boss's violent reaction. I had a hysterical moment to wonder if Fairbanks might try to have us arrested—or shot, for that matter—in hopes of preventing the news from leaving this room.

The reality was much less dramatic. His shoulders slumped, his head dipping as though he suddenly lacked the strength to hold it up. His eyes slid closed.

"I thought I could keep her safe," he muttered, the words barely audible. "God help me, I thought we could keep her a secret."

I nodded to myself, achingly aware of all the new possibilities opening up before us. "I'm sure my parents thought much the same thing," I said. "The question is, what happens to all of the other throwback children whose parents *aren't* powerful and well-connected?"

Fairbanks shook his head helplessly, not looking up. Around the room, I caught several of the bodyguards exchanging uncomfortable glances. I wondered how many of these men had guarded young Samantha Fairbanks as she grew from childhood into adolescence. Had any of them suspected?

"Please sit down, Prime Minister," Nikolayev said. "It appears we do, indeed, have much to discuss."

Fairbanks took a single, heaving breath that lifted and lowered his shoulders. Visibly dragging himself together, he reached down and righted his overturned chair before slumping into it. Elbows on the table, he dug the heels of his hands into his eye sockets for a long moment before he spoke. It didn't matter that he was the elected leader of one of the most powerful federations on the planet. In that moment, he was nothing more than a terrified father.

"I didn't dare act openly against the Committee," he began, letting his hands fall limply to the table, where they lay palm up. "I couldn't risk bringing their attention down on my family."

"How long ago did Samantha present as an omega?" I asked, keeping my tone compassionate.

He gave a mirthless laugh. "Two years ago. She was thirteen. We've had her on blockers and suppressors ever since."

Thirteen. That was young for a first heat—the poor girl.

"And yet, you've still done your best to limit the Committee's power inside the UFNA," I said. "You may not realize it, but you're a symbol of hope to alphas and omegas the world over."

It was shameless flattery. It was also true, in a world where the best we'd been able to hope for was someone to slow the ongoing hemorrhage of our human rights.

Heavy silence fell over the room, broken only by the sound of our breathing.

Fairbanks broke it, his voice emerging as a bare rasp—so unlike his usual commanding baritone. *"It's not enough."*

"No," Nikolayev agreed. "It really isn't. So the question becomes, what are we going to do about it?"

Fairbanks looked like a man gazing into the mouth of hell. "Yesterday… if Jennifer hadn't taken Sammy to the restroom before the gas was released…"

"She could have died at the hands of radical beta supremacists," I finished for him.

He nodded, blank-faced, and then seemed to realize something. "The man who was speaking when the attack started. I recognized him. He used to work with you. Did he survive?"

"He's recovering." I cleared my throat and swallowed, caught off guard by the wave of choking emotion. "Ironically, if the slavers hadn't ripped out his reproductive organs and destroyed his ability to produce omega hormones when he was a kid, he'd be dead like all the others."

Fairbanks stared at me for a long moment. "I can't let my daughter grow up in this twisted excuse for a world."

Hope bloomed in my chest, but I didn't dare trust it yet.

"What do you know of the Beta Liberation Front?" Nikolayev asked.

"I've received intelligence briefings," Fairbanks said dully. "But there's not much information about them. They're a European splinter group, mostly involved in kidnappings and low-level assassinations… at least, until recently."

"And what if I could tie them to Enoch Sloane and his organization?" Nikolayev asked.

Fairbanks' expression sharpened. *"What?"*

"You mentioned kidnappings," Nikolayev replied. "When she was an ambassador, Leona McCready was one of their targets, as you may recall."

The prime minister's gaze flashed to me, and I thought I saw guilt there. "Yes, I do," he said.

"She and her colleagues were successfully retrieved from a stronghold in the Carpathian mountains by a small strike team," Nikolayev continued. "Most of the terrorists were killed in the fighting, but a few got away. Ms. McCready's status as an omega was discovered during her captivity."

I suppressed a shudder, remembering that horrific few days.

"No one else knew her secret besides the terrorists," Nikolayev said. "And yet, a few weeks after her return to Montreal, she was arrested as an unregistered omega after the Montreal police Department received a tip. A tip, I might add, that came directly from a Committee liaison."

Fairbanks blinked at us. I watched as the implication hit home.

He frowned. "That's a tenuous connection at best."

"It is," Nikolayev agreed. "But I have investigations underway to uncover financial links between Sloane and the individual who drugged the drinks at the recent conference in Belarus. Bank records are considerably more useful than hearsay in a court of law."

A fire kindled behind Fairbanks' eyes. "You're telling me Enoch Sloane funded the terrorists who might have killed my little girl?"

"There certainly appears to be a link," Nikolayev told him.

"By god." Fairbanks' right hand closed into a fist. "Get me that proof, and I'll see the pasty-faced Committee rat hauled before an international tribunal before you can say the words *sanctimonious little prick*."

"I would like nothing better," Nikolayev assured him. "And in the meantime?"

"Alphas and omegas are still being bought and sold every day," I said. "Innocent human beings, forced to breed like cattle—or else face involuntary sterilization and second-class status in the eyes of a two-tiered legal system."

"Yes." The prime minister's face settled into sober lines. "Yes—you're absolutely right. I couldn't act before—not unilaterally. One nation can't take on the Committee. But..."

"The Euro-Soviet Committee no longer supports alphomic suppression," Nikolayev finished for him. "I assume there is a question implied in your statement—and the answer is, yes, my branch of the Committee will support you. As will a large bloc of Eastern European and Soviet states."

Fairbanks tapped the fingers of one hand on the table in a thoughtful gesture. "And I think there's growing support among some of the larger Western European states, as well."

"We heard you'd been busy lobbying," I offered. "It sounds like you were already considering an end-run around Sloane and his allies."

He sighed and shook his head. "I wasn't willing to let an upstart terrorist group dictate terms to a meeting of over a hundred nations. Apparently, the fuckers sent in people posing as HVAC maintenance workers to set the gas canisters in place, with remote controls to operate them from a safe distance."

"Practical, I suppose," Nikolayev said blandly.

"As practical as sneaking someone in as a member of the wait staff in Belarus," I added. "I suppose there's no need to be flashy when being pragmatic works so effectively."

"Apparently not." Fairbanks sounded grim. "Very well. If the UFNA were to tackle the subject of alphomic rights in one broad legislative stroke, rather than continuing a policy of lukewarm resistance, what might that look like? I'm open to your thoughts on the matter, Chairman—and yours, Ms. McCready."

I had to take a moment to check in via the mating bond and make absolutely certain this wasn't a dream or a hallucination. Based on Alex and Jax's shocked hope echoing through my thoughts, it wasn't.

"Very well, Prime Minister," I began. "As it happens, we have a package of proposals that we would be more than happy to discuss with you."

TWENTY-FIVE

Leona

WATCHING THE televised perp-walk as Enoch Sloane was led away from his Alabama compound in handcuffs ranked as one of the top three most satisfying experiences of my life. It fell only slightly behind the moment I'd first felt Kam's presence in my mind during the heat when Jax and Flynn had mated us, as well as the moment Alex had finally joined our bond.

Slightly more than six months had passed since we'd met Levi Fairbanks in a hotel conference room and uncovered his most closely guarded secret. He'd been good to his word—risking his tenuous parliamentary coalition by going public with his daughter's omega status... not to mention his intention to lead the world toward a better future where all people received equal rights and protection under the law.

The legislation had been an uphill battle, to put it mildly. There was strong backlash at first, not least from Sloane himself. I'd been utterly convinced that the UFNA progressive coalition would crumble beneath the strain, ushering in something far worse during the next round of elections.

Fortunately for everyone involved, Beckett's deep dive into the financial ties between Enoch Sloane and the Beta Liberation Front had finally hit pay dirt. Confronted with proof that the co-chairman of the Committee was directly responsible for a chemical weapons attack on a gathering of global high-ranking officials, the tide of public opinion turned at a critical moment during the legislative process. Under pressure from voters, the tide of political opinion turned not long after.

Betas had died in that gas attack. Several had been fatally trampled during the mad dash for the exits. A couple more perished of medical complications after the fact—an elderly woman succumbed to a heart attack, and a man died of a burst aortal aneurysm. It was sickening that the deaths of alphas and omegas alone wasn't enough to foster outrage, but there was no denying that the beta casualties had roused public opinion in our favor. Today, we were about to reap the harvest from the seeds of change that we'd sown.

Kam poked his head into the bedroom. "Are you ready, Leo? It's almost time to leave."

We'd been staying in the Russian embassy in Montreal, where Nikolayev's name was enough to secure us a safe haven while the legislative machine ground slowly into motion.

I stopped fussing with my hair and gave myself a final once-over in the mirror. "Yes. Sorry. Just nerves," I said. "Am I holding things up?"

He came in and put his hands on my shoulders from behind. "Not really. I'm just here to give you a five-minute warning."

Clad in a sharp navy suit with a patterned burgundy tie, he looked every inch the suave diplomatic professional. I met his deep brown eyes in the mirror and gave him a tremulous smile.

"This is really happening, huh?" I asked.

He tucked a wayward red curl into place on the back of my head and adjusted a hairpin to keep it there. "Apparently. Though if it's a shared hallucination, at least it's a nice one. Shall we go and join the others?"

"Yes, let's," I said, and took his offered hand.

Tonight, we would witness the presentation of the Alphomic Civil Rights Act to the UFNA Governor General for final approval. If I were more prone to paranoia, I might have become gun-shy about important public functions where large numbers of politicians would be gathering. However, the last six months since the gas attack had seen two vital changes in the world.

First, the Beta Liberation Front's largest source of funding had been cut off, and many of its leaders had been captured or killed. Second, governments had gotten a *lot* more serious about security precautions. Gone were the days when Kam and I had wandered in and out of office parties in the Foreign Affairs building with only a single, bored guard keeping watch at the front door. The Parliament Building—and pretty much every other government installation—had been locked down tight ever since Prime Minister Fairbanks' close call in Luxembourg.

The House of Commons had room for about five hundred spectators in the various viewing galleries above the legislative floor, and it was a fair bet the place would be packed solid. Jax, Flynn, Alex, Kam, and I were attending as Fairbanks' personal guests in the Speaker's Gallery. Beckett and Nikolayev—safely back in Russia with their baby daughter—had declined to travel here and appear in person. They would doubtless be watching the worldwide broadcast on television, despite the seven-hour difference in time zones.

Kam and I exited the bedroom to find the others ready and waiting for us. I'd been prepared for Flynn and Jax in suits, since suits were standard fare in their familiar long-standing roles as bodyguards. I had *not* been prepared for Alex in an evening dress. In fact, I was unprepared enough for Alex in an evening dress that I stopped cold, frozen in place.

She frowned at me. "What?"

I blinked, and then turned my head very deliberately to look at Kam. "You might have warned me about this," I said.

He shrugged, a smile twitching at one corner of his full lips. "I wanted to see your reaction."

Alex was resplendent in a sleeveless, square-neck white satin sheath gown, with her dark hair scraped back in a severe bun. She didn't need makeup to be completely stunning, but I thought I detected a hint of eye shadow, and she was definitely wearing lipstick.

"White suits you," I managed. "And also, Kam and I are going to peel that dress off of you later, so fair warning."

"With our teeth," Kam added helpfully.

Flynn eyed Alex skeptically. "Can you fight in that thing?"

"Probably not without ripping a seam somewhere." Alex didn't look pleased about the admission.

"Maybe we can get through this one official event without imminent danger to life and limb," Jax suggested.

Flynn shrugged. "Maybe. Anyway, we'll be seated in a balcony, so if anyone comes at us, we can just toss 'em over the railing, right?"

"That seems like the simplest strategy," Alex agreed.

I tried not to picture what the newspaper headlines would look like if my alpha bodyguards injured innocent Members of Parliament by dropping terrorists on them from a second-story balcony.

"How about we try to follow Jax's plan of avoiding drama altogether," I said.

A limousine took us to Parliament Square from the Embassy District. The massive Parliament Building was a towering five-story ode to Gothic Revivalist architecture, all stone arches and slender spires, built near the banks of the St. Lawrence River in Old Montreal. We passed through the various layers of security, emerging into the echoing space of the rotunda. Stone and stained glass stretched above us.

The foyer to the House of Commons marked a transition from the churchlike atmosphere of the building's public spaces to the darker, wood-paneled room where the legislature met to carry out the federation's business. It was still a huge room, overlooked by five galleries to accommodate visitors of various ranks and provenance. In here, however, attention was focused downward toward the parliamentary floor, rather than upward and outward toward the marvels of the surrounding architecture.

The chamber smelled of rich leather, dusty paper, and age. It contained all the trappings of ceremonial power—including a red, throne-like chair at one end, where the Governor General would receive Parliament's petition. The sergeant-at-arms directed us to our seats in the front row of the Speaker's Gallery, where we sat, looking down at the spectacle.

The business of the North American government was steeped in tradition, and aspects of it seemed faintly ridiculous to the outside eye. Even in this day and age, there were a lot of robes involved, a lot of rather silly hats, and an awful lot of formal bowing. Every formal communication on the parliamentary floor was repeated in English, French, and Spanish, making things take three times longer than would otherwise be the case.

We watched, sitting through the endless introductions of various officials and clarification of points of order, until finally, a representative of the House of Commons approached the Governor General on her red velvet chair, holding an impressively thick stack of bound paper in front of him like an offering.

He bowed respectfully. "May it please Your Excellency, the Senate and the House of Commons have passed the following bills, to which they humbly request Your Excellency's assent. First, a bill to grant full citizenship and rights to all alphomic individuals within the borders of the United Federation of North America."

The Governor General gave a solemn nod.

"Second, a bill outlawing the practice of slavery, and granting monetary compensation to all individuals held in slavery for their time, labor, and any physical or psychological harm that may have been visited upon them in the course of their subjugation."

Murmurs broke out among the onlookers, only to subside beneath stern looks from the sergeants-at-arms.

"Third, a bill outlawing the involuntary sterilization of any individual, either by chemical or surgical means."

Kam shifted in his seat next to me.

"And finally, a bill lifting all restrictions on the manufacture and sale of drugs and medical devices intended for the treatment of alphomic individuals under a doctor's supervision."

His hand brushed mine and I grabbed it, intertwining our fingers and squeezing hard.

The Governor General nodded again and spoke solemnly, the words too soft to carry to the galleries. I held my breath.

Her spokesperson repeated the words for the onlookers' benefit. "Her Excellency the Governor General thanks the parliamentary representatives, accepts their generous benevolence, and assents to these bills. The Alphomic Civil Rights Act is now the law of the land in North America."

My breath whooshed out of my lungs, leaving me lightheaded as the spokesperson repeated the words in French, and finally Spanish. Around us, tentative applause started up, more and more people joining in despite the fact that it was utterly against protocol inside the House chamber. The five of us clapped as loudly as anyone else. Kam rose to his feet, and so did I—the people around us following

suit until a thunderous standing ovation rat-
tled the room's ancient timbers.

———————◆———————

Hours later, we lay in a naked tangle on the
fur rug in front of the living room fireplace in
our temporary quarters. My hair was sweaty
from exertion. I suspected I had a serious case
of raccoon eyes as a result of smeared mascara,
and I was definitely going to be sore in some
very interesting places tomorrow.

In other words, bliss.

"Can we talk about permanent living ar-
rangements?" Kam asked. He was lying
crosswise with his head in my lap and his legs
thrown over Alex's hips, staring up at the ceiling in the orange, flickering light of the gas
flame.

"Did you have something specific in
mind?" Jax replied, the breath from his words
tickling the side of my neck.

Kam's dark eyebrows drew together
thoughtfully. "I did, yes. When the reparation
payments come through, it's going to mean a
fairly significant lump sum for the pack. Leo
and I will also be putting lawsuits in motion to
recover our confiscated assets, and neither of
us were exactly poor before all of this started."

"You thinking you might want us to buy a
place of our own?" Flynn asked. "Because I
kinda like that idea."

"I was thinking of a very specific place, actually." Kam rolled his head, his dark eyes meeting mine. "What would you say to purchasing the safehouse in upstate New York? The one in the woods."

I mulled that over, not having considered the possibility before now.

"We broke all the windows and singed a bunch of the forest around it with Molotov cocktails," Jax pointed out. "After what happened to us there, I'm surprised the place doesn't hold bad associations for the two of you."

"No," I said slowly. "I mean—yes, those things *did* happen, and they were terrifying. But to me, that house will always be the place where I spent my first heat surrounded by people who I knew cared for me." I paused, and then added, "I really miss that nest."

"*Sex furniture*," Kam offered sagely.

"The sex furniture was pretty good, all right," Flynn said.

Jax snorted. "Well, it's nice to see that everyone's got their priorities straight, anyway."

"What about you, Jax?" I asked. "Does that house hold too many bad memories for you?"

"I'm not sure," he said after a long moment. "I failed you there."

"You didn't," Kam said firmly.

"I couldn't protect you," Jax insisted. "But in the end, Nikolayev capturing us was the only thing that saved us. And... to put things in perspective, absolutely nothing bad happened to us in Nikolayev's guesthouse in Russia. The place was ridiculously huge and ridiculously posh—"

"*Gaudy*," Alex muttered.

"—yet I feel more of a connection to the safehouse in New York than I do to that guesthouse."

I nodded. "Same here. For what it's worth, there will be plenty of time to think about it before we'll be in a position to act."

Alex shifted position, rolling onto her side. "It's a good-sized property. Lots of land, natural surroundings." She hesitated, swallowing. "A good place for pups." The words were quiet and hoarse.

My gaze flew to her. She looked pale in the firelight, but she met my eyes and held them without looking away.

"It *would* be good place for pups," I agreed, imagining a pack of littermates running around in the woods, laughing and climbing trees... playing hide and seek.

Flynn perked up, his smile like the sun coming out from behind gray clouds. "We're gonna have pups soon?"

"Your pups will be beautiful, odama," Kam said.

"*Our* pups," I corrected. "I'm not doing this alone."

Jax had stayed very quiet throughout this part of the exchange. Now he looked up, his blue eyes troubled. "I already have pups.

Probably a lot of them. I know it's not explicitly part of the new laws, but… I want to try and find them, if I can. Assuming any of them want to be found, I mean. There should be records. The breeders were always very particular about pedigrees."

The last sentence sounded bitter in a way that was unusual for my scarred Viking. I squirmed around until I could get my arms around him.

"Of course we'll try. Oh, Jax…"

"Guess there might be a handful out there with my shitty genes, too," Flynn said. "They used me to breed one time, when there was a gap in the rotation. I dunno if she got pregnant or not—they never told me."

"Your genes are not shitty," Kam said, sounding deeply offended. "And I say that as a hoity-toity purebred—so there."

"In fact, your genes are in my 'top three' list of potential sperm donor candidates," I added. "So, don't you dare diss them, or else you're basically saying that I have bad taste."

"Hey—you want my genes; they're yours," Flynn said. "You want any part of me, it's yours. Both of yours."

"Good. In that case, we'll take all of you," I said firmly.

Kam nodded. "Seconded."

Flynn shrugged. "Done."

"Have you made a decision about hormone replacement therapy, once it becomes available?" Alex asked Kam, neatly changing the subject.

The new law meant that as of today, omega-specific drugs were no longer contraband items. Of course, some companies had continued to produce them for the black market even after they'd become illegal—that was how I'd managed to obtain blockers for so many years. But they'd always been scarce, expensive, and of widely varying quality.

Flynn had approached Beckett and Nikolayev a few months ago about finding hormone replacement injections for Kam, but omega hormones weren't readily available on the black market like blockers and suppressors were. With tens of thousands of sterilized omegas gaining full rights and medical compensation for what had been done to them, the drug companies would doubtless smell the potential profits and move to fill that gap in the market sooner rather than later. There was shortly going to be a huge demand for alphomic medical specialists in North America, I was betting.

"Yes," Kam said. "I want to try it. Just so you all realize that it will mean saying goodbye to this carefully cultivated and rather amazing beard, though."

"Baby face," I teased in an obnoxious, sing-songy voice.

He scowled at me. "You have no appreciation for the beard, you philistine," he complained, reaching up to flick me on the ear.

I squeaked in surprise and shoved him off my lap, which somehow devolved into a very uneven five-way wrestling match, and from there, to something much more enjoyable. I hadn't felt so light inside in years. Too bad the Russian Embassy's poor, innocent fur rug was never going to be the same after we were through with it.

EPILOGUE

Leona

Five years later

"*AARGH*! GODDAMN IT, I hate every single fucking one of you right now!" Panting rapidly through my nose, I gritted my teeth until the contraction subsided. My hand ached from gripping Kam's so hard that his knuckles ground together. He wisely didn't complain—or reply. I darted a glance to my other side, a bit sheepishly. "I didn't mean you, Mom. Sorry."

My mother let out a soft snort and gave my other hand a reassuring squeeze. "I'll let it slide this once, Pumpkin," she said. "Let's hope your dad is still keeping the twins occupied outside."

"It's probably not the worst thing they've heard," Kam muttered, *sotto voce*.

Patricia McCready, who had been going by the name Victoria Anderson for the past several years, was the source of my Irish complexion and flaming red hair. Unlike mine, her hair was bobbed short, and also shot through with gray. A patchwork of the kind of freckles that I'd largely escaped dusted her pale skin.

Laugh lines and frown lines decorated her thin face in equal measure. Her eyes were a striking blue, not dissimilar to Jax's.

I was so relieved to have her here with me that I could have wept.

"Give us another big push on the next contraction, luv," said the midwife. "You're starting to crown."

"*Ugh.*" I tried not to focus too much on the fact that this was only the first of two deliveries. If I'd hoped that giving birth to my second set of twins in five years would be easier than the first time around, I was out of luck.

Four familiar presences crowded my mind with love and worry, but I was the only one who could squeeze these pups out. The others would simply have to deal with getting cursed at, both aloud and internally.

"Let's get you up and squatting." The midwife gestured to Kam and my mother. They helped me get in position, despite the fact that my thighs were already shaky from exhaustion.

"Alpha," Kam said softly. "A bit of help over here?"

A moment later, Alex's lean-muscled body settled behind me. Her arms came around me; warm, long-fingered hands resting over my bulge.

"Get ready, odama," she murmured. "Our new pups are almost ready to enter this world and say hello."

I grunted in response, feeling my internal muscles gearing up for another strong contraction. We were in the nest, with its soothing, red-tinged light and mountains of pillows. It was where these pups had been conceived, and where they would take their first breaths. The old house in the woods had been transformed over the past few years. Once a safe haven for alphas and omegas in need, it was now our home.

Our pack house.

As we'd dreamed, the forest outside echoed with the sound of youngsters at play. Matthew and Kristen had been born four years ago, only a couple of months after we'd finalized the purchase of the property and moved in. Kristen had Flynn's unmistakable looks, as well as his stubbornness. Matthew had Alex's green eyes and a hint of red highlights in his dark brown hair. Between them, they'd filled our lives with love and hope for the future.

The overwhelming need to push washed through me, even as my muscles screamed in exhausted protest. I squeezed my eyes shut and bore down, an undignified, high-pitched shriek escaping my throat as things down below stretched past their limits.

I knew that feeling. It was happening—I was pushing the first of our new arrivals out into the world.

"Looking good, Leona," said the midwife. "Just one more push."

Shaking, I clung to the hands holding mine and leaned against Alex's steady strength.

"Almost there, *ma cocotte*," she whispered.

I rallied for a final push, feeling the weight of our new pup slip free, into the midwife's waiting hands. A weak cry came a moment later, followed by a momentary pause, and then a much stronger wail.

"It's a girl," the midwife reported wryly. "And I'm happy to report that she apparently has lungs."

Kam kissed my temple and let go of my hand, taking the little girl in his arms so the midwife could cut the cord. I blinked sweat out of my eyes and looked down at the tiny, scrunched face with something like awe.

"She's beautiful, Pumpkin," my mother crooned, reaching down with her free hand to stroke the downy head. "Do you have a name picked out?"

"Natasha," I said. "She looks like a Natasha, don't you think?"

A single, damp golden curl proclaimed her likely sire.

"Jax will be thrilled," Kam said. "I wonder if she got the blue eyes, too?"

I started to answer, but broke off with a groan when a new contraction hit.

"Here we go again," said the midwife. "Be glad you're not a purebred, or you might have ended up with two or three more left in the chute."

"Have I mentioned that I hate everyone in this room except my mom and my new daughter?" I managed, before the business of delivering Natasha's littermate demanded my full attention.

———◆———

Thirty minutes later, I lay exhausted in a nest of cushions, with baby Dana cradled in my arms. I had two tiny new girl pups, and the contented hum of the pack-bond thrummed in my mind.

Kam sat next to me with his back propped against the front of the overstuffed sectional sofa that surrounded the sunken nest. He'd unbuttoned his shirt, and was trying to get Natasha latched onto a nipple. Dana was already suckling greedily at my left breast.

"There you go, little one," he said, as Natasha finally stopped fussing and started feeding. "Good to know all that time spent in the lactation consultant's office wasn't totally wasted."

Kam had spent the last six months on a hormone and galactagogue regimen to induce lactation, and he had quite a bit to say on the subject of breast pumps these days. He'd been on omega hormone replacement therapy for almost five years now, his body restored to as close to what it might have been as modern medicine could manage.

The beard he'd been so proud of was long gone, and some of the muscle definition he'd worked so hard to maintain was now hidden under a sleek layer of fat. After a considerable amount of research and discussion, he'd opted not to seek reconstructive surgery on his scarred and sealed birthing passage, choosing instead to maintain his existing sexual function, such as it was. The hormones helped, and so did the huge reduction of stress in our lives since the new civil rights laws had gone into effect. The near-constant dark circles were gone from beneath Kam's soulful brown eyes, and his shoulders were no longer knotted with long-held tension.

His presence had ghosted its way into the mating bond a few weeks after he started the hormone regimen. Gone were the days when his connection with us faded following my heat cycles. The five of us were together as we were meant to be—bound in mind, body, and soul.

I'd been the one to prod Kam into seeing the lactation consultant. Even male betas could produce milk with the help of the right drugs. It was considerably more straightforward for an omega. I figured there was no reason why Kam couldn't share the burden of nursing twins this time around. I'd still have to do the bulk of the feeding for the first couple of weeks, since I was the only one producing colostrum. But after that, it would free me up to return to work without the need to rely so heavily on bottles.

It was purely practical, obviously—and had nothing to do with my desire to see Kam with a pup to his chest and love shining from his eyes like a beacon. Nothing at all.

Alex was busy guarding the nest from threats that didn't exist, her green eyes intermittently straying to us with the same dazed, *how-is-this-real* look that I saw on the others' faces from time to time. I could relate. The world beyond our little oasis of peace was far from perfect, or even safe. There were still vocal proponents for beta supremacy and alphomic suppression—the difference was, they were the illegal ones now... not us.

Our cozy pack house in the woods had security cameras and tall fences surrounding it. I still woke sometimes in the middle of the night, convinced that a SWAT team was at the door. But none of us were willing to let the past overshadow the present... or the future. We were mated. We had beautiful pups. We'd helped shape a world that was better than it had been five years ago.

It was enough. Better than enough, it was more than any of us had dared dream.

I felt Jax and Flynn's approach through the bond, and sent a pulse of wordless welcome. The door to the nest creaked open, and our other two mates slipped in, with Krissy and Matt clinging to them like limpets. My father followed a second later.

"Hello," I said. "Come and meet the new family members."

Matt's eyes were very wide as he approached cautiously and looked down at the two red-faced bundles. "Are you okay, Mama?" he asked in a tiny voice. "We heard you yelling."

"I'm fine, sweetheart," I told him, smiling. "Just really tired. Whelping is a lot of work, that's all. You know when Flynn lifts weights, and sometimes he grunts and makes noise when it's extra heavy?"

Matt nodded.

"Well, it's kind of like that," I said.

"Only with added cursing and personal abuse," Kam added helpfully. "Here, do you want to hold your little sisters?"

Kam and my mother helped the two youngsters take their new siblings. Jax and Flynn squatted next to me, pressing kisses against my temple in turn. Then, they staked out spots on the sofa where they could watch the others and wait their turn to hold the pups. My dad took a seat across from us and gave me a critical onceover.

"How are you doing, Leo?" he asked.

I smiled, the expression exhausted but heartfelt. "Never better. I'm so glad you and Mom could make it up. Are you still thinking of moving back to the mainland permanently?"

Krissy perked up. "You're going to live here, Grandpa?"

Dad grinned. "Maybe for half the year, Cupcake. I won't lie—at our age, winters in Jamaica are a lot more appealing than winters in upstate New York."

"Seconded," Kam said. "Can I come and stay with you in the winter?"

I mock-scowled at him. "Traitor."

"Of course you can," my mother said, without a second's hesitation. "Bring the kids with you. We'll play on the beach and drink margaritas while these goofs shiver in the cold."

"I feel like you, as my parents, shouldn't be ganging up on me when I've just given you two new granddaughters," I pointed out.

My mother winked at me. "Oh, very well. I suppose you and your alphas can come along, too."

"Gee, thanks," I told her, without heat.

The new pups had made the rounds while we talked. Alex handed me Dana, while Flynn handed Natasha to Kam. The midwife was busily cleaning things up in preparation for leaving. I dozed a bit, letting the bustle ebb and flow around me, with Dana a comforting weight on my chest and Kam a familiar presence at my side.

Time passed, and Jax nudged me through the bond. "Hey, beautiful," he said, when I blinked back to awareness. The pup in my arms squirmed, yawned, and then settled again.

"What's up?" I slurred, still half-asleep.

Jax held up the cordless phone handset. "Beckett's on the line. I called him to let him know the good news. Want to talk to him for a minute?"

I reached for the phone with my free hand, and he passed it to me.

"Hello?" I said.

"*Hello, Leona.*" The international line crackled with static and distance, but the reassuring voice that had shepherded us through so many crises was unmistakable. "*I just wanted to pass on my congratulations. Kostya sends his regards, as well.*"

"It's good to hear from you," I said, with all sincerity. "How's Anika doing?"

"*Plotting world domination, in between charming every person she meets.*" Humor laced the words. "*The three of us will be in your neck of the woods in a few weeks. I'm hoping we can meet up for a visit. Meanwhile, Kostya is hoping he can pressgang you into helping him woo the German Chancellor into broader concessions on a new pan-European treaty.*"

I groaned. "Tell him to ask me nicely, preferably sometime when I haven't just given birth to twins. But either way, I look forward to seeing the three of you. And as it happens, a group of Jax's pups will be visiting around that time, too. Maybe Anika can keep the rest of them out of trouble for a few hours."

"*Highly doubtful, but it might still be amusing to watch. I'll pass on the message, and we'll let you know when our travel plans are a bit firmer. Get some rest, Leona — it was good to talk to you."*

"And you," I said, before handing the phone back to Jax.

"Let me guess," Kam said, nudging my shoulder. "Nikolayev wants you to charm someone for him?"

"Something like that," I replied, yawning. "Did my parents head out while I was dozing?"

"Grocery shopping," he told me. "They said to make sure you get some proper rest, and they'd take care of provisions for the next few days."

"That sounds amazing." I yawned again, wider this time.

Jax returned, this time without the phone. Alex and Flynn weren't far behind, and they had a freshly bathed pair of four-year-olds in tow.

"Alex says we can nap pack style!" Krissy said.

"That's right," Jax confirmed. "We're all going to welcome your new siblings into the pack. In a few hours, your grandma and grandpa will have dinner for us. Sound good?"

Matt and Krissy nodded solemnly.

"And at some point in the near future, I'll introduce you and your brother to the wonderful world of changing diapers," Kam told them.

"Eww." Matt wrinkled his nose in disgust.

I laughed softly, only to wince as my abused uterus registered a complaint with the management. "Ouch."

"Less talking. More snoozing," Flynn said, arranging the pillows and blankets to make a cozy nest for all of us.

"I'll keep watch," Alex said, settling in.

The others carefully fitted themselves around Kam and me, with our precious burdens sleeping peacefully against our chests. When we were arranged in a warm, comfortable pile, Flynn reached across and smoothed my hair away from my cheek—a tender gesture.

"Love you, Sweet Thing," he said. "You, too, Ginger Tea. And you, munchkins."

I let happiness and contentment flow through me like a warm tide, flooding the bond—feeling it wash back over me, multiplied a hundredfold.

"I love all of you," I whispered. "So much."

"So much," Kam echoed.

The others didn't have to reply aloud. I felt it. We all did. With our pups snuggling against us, I closed my eyes and let sleep slide over me, secure in the knowledge that my family would be here when I woke up.

Pack, forever and always.

finis

If you enjoyed this series, you may also like
Ember Blaze's *All for Knot* duet.